Prismatic

Prose

A

Genre

Bending

Anthology

Copyright 2019 © Colorado Springs Fiction Writers Group
http://www.csfwg.org/

ISBN: 13- 978-1-945632-58-7
Edited by S.R. Battle, Erik Johnson & Robert Bronson
Cover design by Jodi Cox

Editor's Note:

I'm a longstanding member of the Colorado Springs Fiction Writers Group. I've had the pleasure to see all our writers grow and support each other. It's an honor to be involved in this presentation of their creativity. The editing process was challenging and rewarding. My poor eyes may never recover, but that's what trifocals are for. I'm forever thankful to Robert Brownson and Erik Johnson for their helpful insights during the editing process. You're very much appreciated. To all the writers, I may have annoyed the crap out of you, but it was worth it.

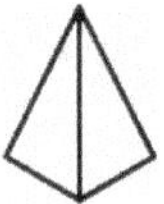

Table of Contents

Nicole Godfrey

Nicole Godfrey is a writer who calls beautiful Colorado home, along with her furry children. She was born in Omaha, Nebraska and has lived in Florida and Tennessee. Her writing started with poetry, leading to her first publication at the age of twelve. She has three short stories published through Colorado Springs Fiction Writers Group: "A Page Lost" in *An Uncommon Collection*, "The Power of the Word" in *Remnants and Resolutions: Tales of Survival*, and "Trials of the Moon" in *Colorado State of Mind*. Her full-length, co-authored titles include *Hoofbeats*, *Chasing the Waves*, and *Open Skies* with AJ Marcus. Nicole actively participates in Amtgard, loves to play table-top RPGs, dabbles in all forms of artwork, and attends college at PPCC.

The Hell That Could Not Embrace Earth

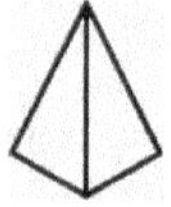

Supernatural Disaster

by

Nicole Godfrey

A loud crack like the clap of thunder shook the ground. Alarms sounded from a multitude of vehicles. Streetlights flashed. Trees shook without the aid of a breeze. And thousands of birds took wing from their perches.

On the summit of Mount Olympus, in the gilded chambers belonging to the Father of the Gods, Zeus roused from a fitful sleep. An ache in his chest echoed the pain of something much deeper. Unease seeped into his bones, and he summoned Hermes with the snap of his fingers.

"How may I serve?" Hermes appeared through a soft glow with a flutter of wings. He bowed at the waist, mahogany curls spilling forward to shroud his youthful face.

Zeus rose from his bed with a ripple of muscle, silken covers falling aside with the wave of his hand. "Something vexes me and keeps me from my slumber." He ran two fingers over his mustache and down his trimmed beard. His ebony hair showed no signs of gray, except some peppering at his temples.

"How troublesome. Do you know its origins?" Hermes kept both his tone and expression neutral as he straightened.

"Indeed I do not, or I wouldn't have summoned you at such an hour. Go forth. Find the source and return to me with word." Zeus waved his hand in dismissal.

"But my lord, I--" Hermes shuffled from foot to foot in midair.

With another wave of his hand, Zeus cut off his son's words. "You are my messenger, with free access to all realms. You will find the problem and return to me."

Hermes inclined his head and disappeared in another globe of light.

Zeus turned and paced the length of the room, summoning his robes to replace the simple wrap he donned for sleep. He wished to return to his rest, but the ache in his chest refused to abate. He went to the large basin, one of many he kept in the palace of Olympus, and waved his hand. The surface rippled as if a drop of water had disturbed the still surface of a pond. An image coalesced, showing him birds darkening the skies of the mortal world with their sheer numbers. The skies were an unnatural shade of inky gray behind them.

The widespread use of technology made it difficult to see major cities through his Eyes, one of his more clever creations, but every location that he turned his attention to seemed to be in the flux of mass chaos. No matter the region of the world, no matter the time of day, people were filling the streets and adding their confusion to the hysteria.

Another tremor shook the entire planet. Zeus gripped the basin as it sloshed and grabbed his chest once more as pain flared. With a thought and a flash of light, he moved to the cavernous throne room in the heart of the palace. Dust cascaded down from the marble columns to mingle with the clouds floating in through the open walls. The sun, even when night moved over the lands below, should've greeted him with its warm glow. Instead, the same inky gray cloaked the skies beyond his home.

The basin here was the largest and represented the world in its entirety. Built into the floor, the Eye could be used by multiple viewers at one time and had the ability to focus on the minutest of details. When not in use, the surface showed the topography as well as the current weather. At the moment, it showed clouds covering the entire globe, which should've been impossible.

"I see you have already been made aware." Apollo, clad in his golden suit of armor and matching flowing cape, stepped through the rolling clouds billowing in through the open columns and bowed.

"Where is your light? Why does it not shine on the mortal realm?" Zeus said in greeting.

"I held out hope you would be able to answer that very question. My radiance has been denied to the realm since before the tremors began. In no part of my domain can I see to the lands below. This vexes me." Apollo unknowingly echoed his father's recently spoken words as he approached and looked down. His golden head still radiated an inner glow, but even that light didn't reach the chiseled features of Apollo's face as it should.

Zeus swept his hand to indicate the basin. "So it does for me as well. We need to find the truth of this, and soon. You are the God of Truth, find for me what vexes us both, that we may be vexed no longer." Zeus waived in the same direction in which Apollo had appeared.

The golden God stood in place, staring at his father.

"Send your beloved creatures if you must, the dolphin and the crow. Call upon your children and any other means you have at your disposal. I fear time is against us and pray we need not call on *him* for aid." Zeus made a conscious effort not to call on Cronos, named for his father, the titan, unless he had no other choice.

With a simple nod Apollo stepped back into the swirling clouds and disappeared.

"You expect someone else to bring you all the answers you seek. A brash move, even for you, brother." Poseidon rose from a swell of water on the floor beside Zeus.

Keeping his eyes on the spot Apollo had occupied, Zeus placed his hand over the ache in his chest. "They are my children and quite capable of a good many things." He turned then. "Am I to assume the same worry brings you before me?"

"Indeed. My oceans are being affected just as much as the rest of the human world. Some malady is spreading like a blight. If not stopped, there will be no end to its impact." Poseidon moved to stand in Zeus' line of sight. The deep folds of his brother's robes resembled the different depths of Poseidon's realm. Midnight blue at his feet, aquamarine toward the shoulders, with material that hinted of both water and stone.

Zeus sighed heavily. "Do you think me daft enough not to know the import of such events?"

"What do you know?" Poseidon asked by way of response.

He waved a hand toward his older brother. "I know enough. With every tremble the earth shutters, a pain of equal measure assaults me. What I need to know is why. What has happened to make the ground shutter?"

"What indeed. How many of your children have come?" Looking down at the basin beneath the floor, a soft glow emanated in the depths of the Sea God's eyes, as if they reflected the swirling clouds covering the Eye.

"Hermes is gathering information, and Apollo says his light can't pierce those clouds." Zeus moved up beside Poseidon and surveyed the floor, as if worried his brother would catch something he himself did not. "Has anything come through the seas perhaps?"

Poseidon's eyes widened ever so slightly, but he didn't look away from his vigil. "If anything had, my brother, I would share. All I know is the deepest parts of the world are reaching toward the surface. The fiery heart of the planet itself is reaching for a reason. We need to find one before she does."

"What do you suggest?" Zeus maintained his pride by being the one to have all of the answers, but this was not the time for pride.

Poseidon finally turned away from the swirling clouds to regard his brother with raised eyebrows. "You have the most intricate network in existence. Use it."

Barely keeping from utilizing the contemporary use of the eye roll, Zeus turned away from his brother and stalked toward his throne. "I expected more from the Lord of the Sea. Of course I'm using my network." He flung up his hand to dismiss the implication of ignorance.

"Are you then?" The tone of Poseidon's voice caused Zeus to abruptly turn on his heel.

Zeus' slightly taller, albeit less muscular, brother put up his hands in a show of surrender to stave off a verbal assault. The folds of his robes billowed out from his body with the motion of a wave. "Peace, brother. I only mean you have yet to call your children home. Bring them here and get the information firsthand."

Thunder and lightning accentuated the roiling clouds surrounding Olympus. Zeus wanted very much to remind his brother who the Father of the Gods was, and his temper bordered on loss of control. The last thing he wanted, aside from the destruction of his beloved mortal realm, was all of the lesser Gods and Goddesses together in one place. He'd lose the advantage of intimidating the masses.

The two immortals stayed locked in a battle through their gazes. Poseidon remained calm and steady, not trying to win, but refusing to give footing. Zeus silently cursed his brother's unwavering patience, knowing full well he'd lose the staring contest and not wanting to waste the time to try. The last bout had lasted centuries, finally being broken by Hermes delivering the news of a near cataclysmic ice age. Zeus blinked with a heavy sigh.

"I suppose your suggestion has merit, as much as I hate to admit it. My children can prove quite unruly when all in one place. Almost as if they get along better if they forget the rest exist." Feeling the weight of stress settle between his shoulder blades, Zeus rubbed the back of his neck.

The ghost of a smile softened the cold lines of Poseidon's chiseled jaw. "So weighs the burden of bearing children, immortal or not."

Zeus managed a laugh at the bone-deep truth. "So it is."

The hard set of Poseidon's expression returned, and he bowed at the waist. "I will leave you to your summons and will return when the last of your children arrive." He turned in a swirl of deep blue that convalesced into a small wave as the Lord of the Sea sank back into the floor.

A slight weight lifted from Zeus' shoulders. Every time he was around either of his brothers, knots formed almost instantaneously in his muscles. He shivered as he thought of Hades. Banished to the Underworld, Hades had become distant and uncaring to matters of the world. Even after Persephone joined him, the Lord of the Underworld still couldn't be counted among the happy souls, made evident by the overly accentuated decrepit physique Hades chose to appear in. Zeus vowed to save that particular summons for last.

As if he'd waited for Zeus to be alone, Hermes appeared in a flash of light and his signature flutter of wings. Said wings folded against the golden sandals strapped to Hermes' feet. He bowed deeply to Zeus.

"My lord and father."

"Ah, Hermes. You return to me quickly. Impart some revelation that may lift the pain from my chest." Zeus held out his arms to his son.

Hermes nodded and stepped closer, but remained outside of Zeus' reach. Slowly, the Father of the Gods lowered his arms. He pardoned his children when they spurned his affections, being that they were normally given to young and beautiful women.

"I wish I could bring you the news you long for. But Father, the tidings are ill no matter where you look for them. None of the other Gods or Goddesses, none of your children, can access their ties to the human world." Hermes stated in a somber tone.

"Ah," Zeus said. "As I feared, we are losing our influence because of this calamity. Very well, begin the summons of all the immortals and their blood-tied demigods."

With eyes still downcast, Hermes leaned into another bow and turned to leave. Zeus caught his arm before he could disappear again.

"For the sake of us all, leave Hades for last. Do you understand?" Zeus spoke low, gripping the inside of Hermes arm with urgency.

The pale green of Hermes eyes glinted in the soft light as he finally looked up. "Of course. I will do as you command."

"Good, my son. You serve with the same loyalty as ever. Be prepared. Should the situation grow more dire, drastic measures may need to be taken." Zeus released his grip and patted Hermes' arm. "Now, go with all speed."

The Messenger of the Gods turned into a glimmer of light and vanished from sight. Another tremor rocked the foundations of the earth and Zeus collapsed to one knee. Should the crust of the earth give way, he wasn't sure his heart could withstand the repercussions. With a thought he returned to his chambers, taking his time to rise to his feet before walking to his personal Eye. This one differed in one very specific way. The focus it had centered on the mortals he had ties with. He tried to direct its gaze toward his current infatuation, but the gray veil refused to allow a viewing. As usual, he'd taken his time to watch her, to learn her, and this time his diligence proved a downfall. He may never see her again.

Sadness joined the pain in his chest. Old habits die hard, and Zeus could be considered the origin of that overused statement. He shook his head, refusing to concede defeat until he'd exhausted every last option.

A knock on his chamber door brought Zeus out of his troubled thoughts.

"Enter!"

Before the door swung outward, Zeus stood to face Hermes, wondering why his son had returned so soon. Hermes entered, gaze scanning the ground like it held some great secret. The messenger's shoulders slumped inward and his skin tone seamed more pale than normal.

Standing as straight as the pain would allow, Zeus motioned Hermes forward. "Unburden yourself and tell me what ails you, my son."

Hermes stepped into the air, the wings on his sandals unfurling and keeping him aloft. "I have more ill tidings. After delivering the decree for all to gather in the meeting hall, I tried to enter the Underworld to deliver the decree to Hades and Persephone. I was immediately ejected from my transition."

Holding up a hand, Zeus stayed the flow of words. "Tell me how this is possible. You are able to slip from realm to realm, at any time and at any location."

Waiting for Zeus' gesture to continue, Hermes swallowed and resumed his tale. "I tried several times, to no avail. When I searched for the truth of the block, I found out the worst has happened."

Realization came as swiftly as one of Zeus' own thunderbolts. His mind tilted dangerously, threatening to unbalance his very existence at the implications. Hermes glanced up and then quickly looked away.

"So, he finally did it." Zeus rubbed his brow.

"Yes, my Lord, Hades has finally managed to succeed." Hermes floated before his father, head bent.

"Why now? What changed?"

"My Lord?" Hermes hovered closer.

"What gave him the push he needed to go the final step? He spoke of moving the Underworld to another dimension for a millennium." Zeus paced in front of his vacant bed, reminding him of the rest he'd been disturbed from.

"Other than the worsening conditions on Earth, I know not of why, my Lord." Hermes clutched his hands together as the Father of the Gods prowled in front of him.

"Attend the gathering. Let none deny you as you act in my stead till my arrival. Go, now." With a wave of his hand, Zeus dismissed his messenger once more. Hermes nodded and sped off at top speed.

The Lord of Olympus left his chambers, the animated heavens on the ceiling darkened with roiling clouds at his passage. Thunderclouds built with the pressure of his worry. Lightning arced randomly and lit the echoing hallways. After several twists and turns, Zeus arrived at his destination. He'd taken the time to walk in order to think.

"Come in, dear husband." The dulcet tones of Hera welcomed him before he could raise a hand to knock.

"You expected my arrival." Without a single touch, the door swung in and Zeus stepped through.

"Of course. What kind of Goddess would I be if I missed the footsteps of my beloved approaching?" She faced away from him, gazing out over the storm shrouded sky.

"You always did have a special sense for my needs." A smile formed on the chiseled features of his face.

"And you have always had a way of manipulating me into doing what you wanted. What is it that troubles you now?" Her slender fingers glided over the silky feathers of a peacock, sitting beside the Goddess on a pillow.

"May it trouble you to learn that Hades has taken the Underworld and moved it to a new plane of existence?" A schooled mask of emotionless features settled over Zeus's face.

Hera's head snapped up, eyes flashing like quicksilver, and fixed the man before her in a steely gaze. Her flawless skin and perfectly quaffed hair could've been hewn from marble. Even her shapely lips showed no sign of smudging in their crimson stain. Had she not slept at all?

"Treason. Betrayal. How will souls find their way to the afterlife? Purgatory will overflow and the dead shall walk the earth." Hera stood, spilling her pet to the floor as it gave a startled cry.

"Yes, which is why I called a gathering."

"You would remove our presence from the mortal plane? Even for a short while? The insanity continues!" Green and blue folds of gossamer cloth billowed around Hera with the sway of her shapely hips, even as her anger crackled in the air. Standing nearly as tall as Zeus, Hera met her husband's gaze evenly as she crossed her arms.

"What choice do we have? The effects of what my brother has done reverberate in the very bones of reality. A decision must be made, and now. This move will tip the balance into chaos, and there are far too many planes for me to search. By the time I brought him back, it would be too late." The air thickened with tension. Energy sizzled as the two immortals stared at each other.

"I accept that you may be right. However, I wish to remind you that the human race you love so much will surely fall. Will you stand by while that happens?" She stepped closer still, her head tilting to the side in an elegant gesture of challenge.

Zeus' gaze cast down, the muscles of his jaws flexed rapidly, and he balled his fists at his sides. Then he brought his gaze back to his wife. He straightened his back, shoulders leveled, and looked into Hera's marble hardened face.

"I will do what I must in order to preserve our way of life. Even if that means abandoning my wayward children and moving us elsewhere to rule." A shiver rode down his spine at the thought.

A smile tugged at the lips of his Queen. She nodded and the tension broke in the form of a thunderclap.

"To the lower chambers then, my love." She swept from the room with Zeus hot on her heels, a flash of light consuming them the moment they crossed the threshold.

When they arrived in the bowels of Mount Olympus, the doors to the massive meeting chamber stood open. The din from so many voices made conversation impossible, but still the throng murmured. Silence fell and all eyes focused on the couple who ascended the dais. Hermes hovered nearby, the only other God to stand out from the masses.

"My family. It has been many years since we all stood in this room. Unlike that time, today we gather to discuss our future. Hades, my brother and Lord of the Underworld, has taken his dominion and moved it to another plane. This will inevitably throw the mortal realm into chaos. Finding him and bringing him back in time to stop this from happening is not an option. So I ask, should we leave the mortals to their fate and find a new home? Or should we stay and face what is to come?" At first there was no response, and then the din that followed shook the walls of the great mountain almost as severely as the tremors plaguing the surface of the mortal world.

"Silence!" The thunderclap of Zeus' voice echoed through the skies surrounding Olympus. When the noise abated, he continued. "I will make this easy. You will use your voices to cast your vote. The answer that gets the greatest response determines our course." He looked to Hera, who stood aside with a haughty smile upon her face, and then back to his kin.

"We stand at the ready, my lord." Hermes said.

"All those in favor of staying?" Again, the sound shook the walls and brought a smile to the face of Zeus. "All those wishing to leave?" His smile disappeared as the din caused dust and rock to shake loose from the stone above. "Very well. Go now, you may bring nothing of this world other than what is upon you."

With his final words, a massive gate opened in the rock wall with a harsh grinding. Slowly, the Gods and Goddesses, accompanied by their blood-tied demigods, left their home. Zeus and Hera left last, walking hand in hand for the first time in an age.

Right before the gate sealed, a glimmer of light surged through and back into the meeting hall. Hermes stepped out in a flutter of wings and smiled as the gate disappeared and left only solid rock once more. He fluttered up to the open throne room and landed before the great Eye covering the floor. With a wave of his slender hand, he banished the clouds from a small area and peered down at the mortal realm.

Down on earth, a hand clawed its way up through the ground as the first of the dead rose from their slumber. More followed at a cumulative rate. They would cover the globe soon enough.

"None of those fools even guessed. Not one." Hermes held

out his hand as a black swirl of liquid shadow solidified beside him. Persephone stepped out and closed her fingers around his. "And I would never have succeeded without you."

A smile curled her ruby lips and she bent her head to place a kiss on Hermes' knuckles. Not a trace of her summer persona remained, hair and eyes dark as ebony against the alabaster of her skin.

"What of Hades, my love?" he asked, barely keeping himself from pulling her against his body.

Her breath caught, as if she knew his thoughts. "He busied himself with the move so fully that he never even noticed my absence until it was too late."

"Now you will rule by my side, where you belong. But first, we let the dead do their job. When the dust settles, the remaining human population will fall at our feet when we banish the dead to a new hell." He looked her up and down, licking his lips with greedy desire.

"And you are sure none of the Gods and Goddesses can return, not even Zeus?" As usual, Persephone managed to inject enough doubt into her words to rile Hermes' anger.

He did pull her against him then, crushing her smaller frame to fit into his. "I made sure of it. The seal was set by Zeus himself, but also enforced by Hera." He kissed her and bit her lower lip until she whimpered. Only when she panted for breath did he pull back, growling with satisfaction. "Now, shall we enjoy the show?"

Courtney Fisher

Courtney is originally from Los Angeles and has been writing short stories and novels since he was eight years old. He has been a member of the CSFWG since 2017. He writes in a variety of genres, primarily focusing on young adult fantasy and science fiction. Courtney currently lives in Colorado Springs where he attends the teacher education program at UCCS. When not writing, he enjoys walking the mountains of Colorado and exploring the many sights and locations of the colorful state.

The Cave

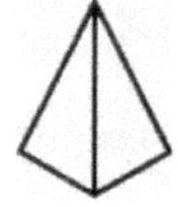

Western Cosmic Horror

by

Courtney Fisher

I came to the town of Spiral Sky for the same reason everyone else did. I came chasing rumors of a legendary deposit of silver up in the Rocky Mountains. I think those who heard the call were mostly like me: no families to take care of, wandering the country in search of work, and taking opportunities that came to us. I think you had to be that way, because the town was so far out of the way it took a wandering soul to find it. No railway went all the way out to the little settlement, so I had to toss a couple dollars at a rancher to allow me to tag along as he brought his cattle into the area.

When I finally made it, I took in the sight of the one-street town. I could see a general store, a saloon, and a few houses, but everything seemed miniscule compared to the massive green mountains looming above just a mile or so away. They were shrouded in fog, which I found odd. I'd been up and down the

Rockies at one time or another, and the one thing I always noticed was how dry they were. The settlement itself was perfectly dusty and hot, with not a cloud above us. The mountains on the other hand looked positively lush, at least as far as I could see, and the fog had to mean there was moisture up there.

I didn't know whether to be excited or disappointed by the town itself. Those who talked about it always gave it a variation on the same name. "The Dapper Town," "The Foothills of Wealth," and so on. I didn't expect it to look so plain. There weren't that many folks around, certainly nothing to suggest a major mining operation nearby. I must've known a hundred people that knew the story of Spiral Sky. Half as many told me they were out to find the silver, and it was the stuff of common knowledge around camps and otherwise empty train cars.

There were some people around, mind you. As I got closer, I realized how out of place they looked in the dusty old town. They were revealed to be more the kind of people I expected to see given the nicknames the town got. Everybody I saw walking down the street on either side was dressed to the nines and oozed money. Nice suits, elegant dresses, the finest breeds of horses each with good weight and muscle to them. Everyone was groomed and carried themselves like they were loitering around the richest part of Manhattan. Some of the buildings matched that motif, too. Once I could see properly, the shops lining the street were all regular enough, but out behind them and up in the hills a bit were some homes that really looked out of place. In fact, they were really more like mansions. They stuck out in their crisp paint and sprawling gaudiness.

A man passed by me, and I saw his jet-black shoes collecting dust as he walked.

"Hey there," I said as he walked by. He just gave me this split-second look of contempt before picking his pace up and hurrying along. These people had the attitudes of those Manhattanites as well. I caught up to a woman in a huge white dress that similarly collected dirt around its edges.

"Ma'am," I said as I walked by. I glanced back to see her reaction was just like the man's: cold and nasty.

All right, I said to myself. To hell with these rich weirdoes. I wondered if it would be better to wait until tomorrow before I went exploring up in the foothills, and perhaps the fog would clear out by then. I still needed to find a place to stay while I prospected anyway, and I was famished to boot. I was drawn to the saloon by and by, so I made my way across the dusty road clutching my battered old suitcase full of gear.

I made my way in and was greeted by the smell of stale tobacco and alcohol. It was mostly empty, except for a few people up at the bar and a gentleman by himself in the corner. The bartender looked at me as I walked through the door and shut it behind me. It was oddly quiet inside, and I headed straight for the bar, only to hear a voice out of that lonely corner.

"Mister," the man said. I turned to him. "Won't you join

me?"

I shrugged and walked over to his small table. I set my suitcase to the side and sat down in a nice wooden chair. The man across from me was young, and he was dressed a bit like the folks outside.

"What brings you here?" he asked. His voice was smooth, like a salesman's.

"Prospecting," I said. I didn't want to get too much into detail right away, in case he was looking out for competition. The way he was dressed, he'd already done just fine.

"Heard about the great heaps of silver, huh?" he continued. He was fishing around, after all.

"Yup," I said, and then hoping to deflect any suspicion, continued. "Think it might be just a rumor though. These things usually are."

"Oh, it's quite real," he said at once. "It's just that folks come through here all the time looking for it, but scarcely do they stumble upon anything of note up there. It's real hard to find."

"All the more reason to think it's fake," I said. "Mayhap it's just a legend. What makes you think otherwise?"

"I went up on a trip with a prospector once," he said, leaning in and lowering his voice. "We found part of it. He mined out all he could carry and gave me some of it. Only he wouldn't let me see any of the maps. Think he didn't want me talking about where it is."

"So it's all gone, then?" I said, deflated.

"Nah, nah, didn't say that at all. He left for his home to go quietly sell the stuff. Said he was gonna come back for the rest with a proper operation. That was only less than a month ago, so I suspect he'll be back anytime. Now's the time to go get the rest, supposing you can find it."

"Why are you telling me this?"

He leaned back again and shrugged. "I think we ought to spread the wealth around. I got my share and he got his. Now I don't have to work the rest of my life. I guess I just want to pay it forward. In fact, don't tell anybody I said this, 'cause I could get in a heap of trouble when that prospector comes back, but those two fellas over there," he gestured at the bar, where sat an old man and his younger companion. "They showed me a map they got, and I think they're just about on the money from what I remember. I spoke with them earlier. Friendly guys. I bet they'd let you come along with them."

I looked at the men at the bar. They looked nice enough, I supposed.

"Thanks," I said. "What's your name?"

"David," he said. "And yourself?"

"John," I said, standing up. Before I could leave, he reached out with lightning quickness and grabbed my arm.

"Listen," he said. "Just keep your wits about you and leave at the first sign of trouble. Strange things happen up there sometimes. Don't get greedy. I mean it."

I didn't know what to say to that, so I just stared at him. He let go of my arm, and then partially got out of his seat to address the bartender.

"His first one's on me, Tom," he yelled across the room. Tom the wrinkled bartender nodded silently back.

I grabbed my suitcase and headed for the bar, taking the seat next to the old man David had pointed out. I slung my suitcase under the stool.

"Hi there," he said cheerfully.

I turned to look at him, and saw that he was actually middle aged, and he bore coveralls and a bright smile under his scraggly beard. Next to him was the younger guy, who I now guessed was all of about twenty.

"Hello," I offered in return. Maybe I didn't sound enthusiastic, but I was growing more tired and thirsty.

"What brings you out here?" he asked, his tone unaffected by my apathy.

"Prospecting," I said. I turned to the bartender, but before I could ask for anything, the chipper guy spoke up again.

"Ooh, going to look for the silver deposit, huh?" That got my attention.

"Yeah," he continued. "Legend has it there's more silver up there than the rest of the state put together. I don't suppose you believe in all that?"

"I believe," I said. "Can't be that much smoke without a fire."

"Well," the man said. "Happens that Wiley here and I are off lookin' for it, too."

"I heard," I said, unsure how I should respond to that.

"Oh?"

I nodded and pointed a thumb over my shoulder. "From David over there. He said he talked to you."

"Spoke to David, huh? Guess he's gone and left already. Nice man."

I looked behind me, and sure enough, the corner was empty.

"Won't you have a whiskey with us?" the man pressed. "They got damn good stuff here."

"I don't drink anymore," I said a little sheepishly. Seeming like an appropriate transition, I addressed the bartender at last.

"Do you have any coffee?" I asked.

The old bartender behind the counter gave me a look, and then answered in an ancient, gruff voice. "S'pose I can put on a pot."

"Thanks," I said, looking down at the weathered, stained wood of the bar.

"You know," the man next to me said. "I find it awful hard to prospect without any liquor in me."

I nodded absently. "I'm not really experienced," I admitted. "I mean, I've done a few trips. But never been that successful."

"Well, what drawn you to hunt for this particular silver, then?"

I shrugged. "Guess I'm just tired of living in camps. I want a place of my own. Seems like this is as big a score as they come."

"Maybe you'd be better off coming with us, then," the young man, Wiley, said.

"S'pose that's not a terrible idea," the other man said. "There are bears and mountain lions up there, did you know that? You got a piece on you?"

Truth was, I didn't. I couldn't afford one. "No," I said. "I have a knife and my pickaxe, but not much more than that."

"That won't work on any o' those beasts up there," the man warned. "Wiley's right, maybe you best come along with us. If the legend is true, there's more than enough bounty to go around."

David was right after all. These two were welcoming me with open arms. In fact, they seemed like the kind of guys to get into trouble by being too trusting. "I'll only come if it's not a bother," I said. "I'd hate to inconvenience the two of you."

"Don't you even worry about it!" the man said sincerely. "We're glad to have you. I'm Pete, by the way."

"John," I responded, shaking his hand. The bartender returned with a piping cup of black coffee. I had a modest amount of money to sustain me, but it wouldn't last long. I was grateful not to have to pay for this delicious smelling cup. It tasted bitter, but I felt a boost that I sorely needed, nonetheless.

"What brought you guys out here?" I asked.

"Same as you, really," Pete said. "'Cept we've got some

experience already." He chuckled and polished off his whiskey. "We've been working together for a few years at least. We're able to carry our weight mos' of the time.

"I'm sure you know better than me," I said. "I'm just hoping to make enough to get a place of my own someday." I took an overly large sip of the scalding coffee and gasped involuntarily at the heat.

Well," he responded, clapping me on the shoulder. "We're gonna head out in the morning, and maybe we can come back to town loaded up with enough haul to take care of all of us for a long while. You got a place to stay for tonight?"

"No."

"Well, we got ourselves a room upstairs," he gestured up at the ceiling. "It ain't much, but I'm sure you can camp out on the floor if you want."

That didn't sound ideal, but to avoid paying for a room was never a bad thing. It wasn't like I was swimming in money. Maybe that was why the kind man had offered. I accepted after some more back and forth, and as the day wore on we talked until we grew tired. Pete and Wiley told me about themselves, and how they had a knack for prospecting that was scarcely rivaled by anyone else here in the Colorado foothills.

After a time, we retired upstairs, and the two of them were kind enough to loan me a blanket for the night. I slept pretty peacefully, given the circumstances, huddled up under the thin quilt and resting my head on my leather suitcase.

The Cave

The following morning, we set out with the rising sun at our backs. The mountains were still foggy, and I wondered if that would ever clear up. Pete and Wiley were fully equipped with gear and food for a couple weeks. I was still a little suspicious of their incredible good will. Why would they consent to share such a treasure as the largest silver concentration in the state? I kept my eyes on the two of them, David's words in mind.

Perhaps I wasn't very perceptive, but these two just seemed to be genuinely kind individuals. Or maybe they'd grown to want someone else to talk to on long prospecting trips. Either way, we spent the whole morning hiking up in the foothills, following the sketched map of the area that David told me about.

Morning became afternoon, and then twilight. Along our path up into the misty mountains, we discovered copious evidence of prospecting camps, including old shreds of tents, tools, and firepits. Clearly, this was at least close to the place we wanted to be.

We stopped for the night after it grew to be far too dark to navigate safely. My two companions had brought two fairly large tents with them, and Wiley explained that they normally slept separately. Since I was there, they insisted I take the second one, as the first was comfortably large enough for two. Feeling guilty at the prospect of taking up one of their tents, I protested. They would hear none of it, especially not Pete, whose niceness was so intense it was a wonder he'd made any money at all in this business.

That said, it was hard not to let my guard down after a while. Thoughts of treachery and suspicion fell away after that first night when I awoke safely with the morning. Pete set about making a stew for us in the misty morning before we set off again, in a different direction this time. He justified this as "a hunch", interpreting his map differently. According to Wiley, such guesses had a tendency to produce good results.

It was about midmorning when we finally came across something interesting: a large cave in the side of a rocky face. It was heavily obscured by trees, and we almost didn't notice it. In fact, we passed within ten feet of the entrance before we fully realized what it was. There were tools and other camp signs absolutely littering the area, ranging from the freshly abandoned to those rotted by many years. There were no active tents, though. This area seemed to be quite lonely right at the moment.

The mouth of the cave was huge, easily able to accommodate several men and maybe a horse side by side. It was incredibly dark inside and sent a powerful shiver up my back as I looked into the deep blackness. I was all set to move on, but Pete wanted to take a look inside.

"Not sure that's a good idea," I warned, thinking of what I'd been told the previous day. "Could easily be bears in there."

Wiley sided with his longtime companion. They reasoned that the deposit might be in there. Perhaps, they said, that's what kept others from the legendary cluster. I refused to join them, as my bad feeling insisted I get nowhere near it. So I told them I'd keep guard outside, and they relented after poking fun at me.

Having left the majority of the gear with me other than an oil lantern, they headed in. I lost sight of them almost immediately in the blackness of the hole, which seemed to swallow the light. For several tense minutes, I watched the mouth of the cave for them to return, and kept my ears pricked for screaming or the rush of escaping feet. Nothing. No horrifying sound drifted from the deepness. I set about to find a suitable place to take a seat among the prickly grasses and small inconspicuous cacti.

I found a nice smooth rock to rest on a ways off, and thankfully it still gave me a full view of the cave. As I sat, I hoped the trip wouldn't end in disaster on its second day. David's warning came to mind. *Leave at the first sign of trouble.* After ten minutes of introspection, something glinted powerfully in the sunlight that made its way between the thick trees that swayed every so often in a stiff breeze. I tracked it to its source, and jumped to my feet.

There, right in front of me, was a vein of silver poking out of a strangely shaped rock formation. A significant amount was visible, so I could only dream what lay beneath. I almost reached into my suitcase for my pick but stopped. I knew I should retrieve my companions first. I headed uncertainly to the dark entrance of the cave and called within. No sound returned save my own echo, and my skin crawled.

I yelled again, as loud as I could muster. No one answered,

and my nerves were acting up. Thoughts drifted through me about what kind of fate they might've met within the great cave. I was trying to steel myself, growing convinced something bad happened to them, when I heard the faint, unmistakable sound of footsteps on the stone. They were slow and measured, but set me on edge nonetheless. My imagination went wild as I moved backward instinctively, conjuring images of cannibalistic natives emerging holding the heads of my companions.

Then two shapes formed out of the blackness, drawing closer and closer from the dark. Pete and Wiley emerged in due course, looking less cheery than usual but not worse for wear. The lantern they had brought in there was missing.

"Hey!" I called to them, never happier to see a pair of gentlemen I barely knew. They looked at me, but their expressions were strangely muted and distant. "I found a vein up here! Sticking right out of the ground and everything!"

That seemed to rouse them. They joined me, and I showed them my accidental discovery. They marveled at it similarly to how I had, and we set to work on it in due course. It wasn't very tainted, and actually seemed almost pure. I could barely believe it. It looked as if the legend was true after all! I asked Pete about what they found in the cave, hoping to hear that they found more within. He was noncommittal in response. He said that the lantern slipped and broke when they were a little ways in, so they couldn't see much.

My imagination was going wild again, but now with the

thoughts that maybe there were heaps of ore in there, maybe even nuggets as well given how pure this silver up top seemed. I voiced this to the two of them, and strangely they both indicated they'd rather look on the surface. I couldn't believe the sudden change in attitude and got the distinct impression that something happened in there that they didn't want to talk about.

Still, we'd struck pay dirt. We made a more permanent camp just a hundred yards or so from the cave, and I set about helping Wiley gather firewood. Storm clouds were approaching, so we wanted to get supper going before it was too late. They warned me to keep in my tent when I could see lightning, but I knew better than to be caught in the open during a thunderstorm anyway.

I tried to make conversation with Wiley, high spirited as I was, but he just seemed to want to chop and haul wood back to camp in silence. I asked him if anything happened to them in the cave, and he just told me he got afraid of the dark. Odd, of course, since he'd gladly volunteered to go in there with naught but an oil lamp. I let it go though, and soon we had a pretty good fire going back at camp. Dinner was bread with beans, and we headed to bed early as the rain started. It was just a sprinkle at first, but soon deteriorated into a full-blown storm, complete with cracks of thunder so close they rattled my teeth and stood the hair up on my head.

Sometime late in the night, I was awakened by an almighty *BOOM*. I was up in a sitting position within a split second, breathing hard. I knew it was just lightning, and right on cue another flash lit up my whole tent. In the white light I saw the large still shape of a man silhouetted against the canvas side. My heart stopped for a second, and I grabbed for my knife and held it tightly. I scooted toward the flap and pushed it gingerly to the side, unsure what I was planning on doing.

As I squinted into the pouring rain, I couldn't see anyone near. There was certainly nobody standing right over my tent. I calmed down a little and wondered if I'd just dreamed it. Maybe I was still partially asleep when I imagined the shadow.

Lightning flashed again, close enough to leave another echoing boom following, but somewhat quieter than before. In the sudden light before me there was the person who left the silhouette on my tent. He was far off and seemingly facing away from me. I stepped out of the tent, holding my free hand above my eyes in a vain attempt at shielding them. I walked a few steps toward the still figure, heart pounding again. I was soaked from the first instant I stepped out, and my bedclothes clung to me in unpleasant chilliness. It was impossible to tell who was standing over in the distance, between the darkness and raindrops streaming down my face into my eyes. The rain was hard enough that each impact on my skin stung and sapped the warmth from me. I was still gripping my knife, but I held it inconspicuously at my side in case this was Pete or Wiley.

As I grew closer and closer, the dark figure didn't move a muscle. It was shirtless and shoeless, only wearing a set of pants that flapped in the wind. Whoever it was didn't appear to hear my approach over the howling storm, either. After several agonizing seconds, I recognized the messy crop of Wiley's hair moving in the gusts. I moved with less apprehension then and broke into a jog over the rest of the distance between us. He still didn't turn around.

"Hey!" I yelled over the din of the storm. "What are you doing out here?"

He didn't answer me and remained as unmoving as a statue. As I stepped next to him and saw his face, he was staring blankly ahead over a small canyon. It didn't look like he was blinking, and I shuddered. My eyes were drawn down to his chest, where a mark stuck out on the skin below his neck even in the poor light. It looked like a handprint, black and contrasting with his skin, wrapped around the base of his neck.

"Wiley!" I hollered. "What's wrong? What happened?"

He still didn't answer but looked straight at me. His eyes, unblinking in the sheets of rain, gazed unconcerned at me. He just stared at me, and it seemed like there was sadness, or maybe some kind of fear on his face. It was hard to tell in the inconsistent light. He turned from me and walked back toward the camp, shuffling slowly over the muddy landscape. One more flash of lightning illuminated his back, and then he disappeared in the direction of his and Pete's tent.

I stood there in the rain for a minute, trying to process what just happened. Wiley looked out of his mind, almost like he was sleepwalking. That, or under the influence of some kind of possession. Had he been attacked? It looked like someone had put a hand on his neck hard enough to leave a deep mark. I couldn't think of a good explanation for that, other than he might have gotten into a fight with Pete. Eventually I returned to my own tent, thoroughly soaked and afraid to fall back asleep. His behavior scared me, and left me wondering whether he'd come and visit me during the remainder of the night. I was shaking, but I wasn't sure if it was from fear or cold.

I think I did fall asleep after a long time, because I remember waking up to the morning sunlight shining through the ever present fog and through the tent flap, striking my face. I emerged into the day, horribly tired and still freezing cold. I trudged through the thick mud to the campfire after changing, where Pete was conjuring up another vegetable stew. Wiley was nowhere to be seen.

"Did something happen to you two in that cave?" I asked, deciding in that split second to be completely blunt.

Pete looked up at me, weary. "Nothin'," he said. "What makes you ask?"

"Wiley was out in the storm last night," I said. "Just standing there with this vacant stare on his face. Wouldn't talk to me. Like he was possessed or something."

"He gets like that during bad storms," Pete answered. "Don't rightly know why. I think he had some things happen to 'im in childhood. That's all I'm sure of."

I supposed I could accept that. "And he had this mark on him. Like a handprint."

"That ain't none of your concern, John," Pete said. "He's got a history he don't like to talk about. Please let it alone."

"I was thinking," I said, moving on. "About heading into the cave myself. You know, to see if I can find some ore with proper lighting."

Pete's head snapped up at that. His expression was strange and alarming, full of both fear and excitement. "No!" he said loudly, but then softened his tone. "There ain't nothing in there. It's dangerous. We 'bout fell into a huge chasm. That's how we lost our lantern. I don't know how deep it is, but you just know you'd never be found if you went snooping in there."

"Good lord," I said, imagining a great hole in the dark, leading all the way down to hell. I didn't like Pete's reaction, but I supposed he was just a little shaken after nearly falling in like he said.

Wiley came back around by and by. He was talking again, which was good, but he wouldn't address what happened the night before. I never noticed before, but his shirt covered all the way up to his neck, so that mark wasn't visible. Had he always dressed like that? We got to work on the area where we had found the first vein. Streaks and stripes of silver ran deep in the surface rock, and it was clear we'd hit a jackpot. By the end of the second day, we figured to have over a hundred full ounces in strikingly pure ore. It was everything I'd hoped for so far, but the atmosphere was less than jubilant.

Both Pete and Wiley remained friendly enough, but their kindness didn't feel as genuine as it had when I'd first met them a couple days earlier. Their words felt forced, and I caught them every now and again sneaking meaningful looks with each other, or else glancing from side to side as if expecting to be attacked.

It went on like that for days. The spot in front of the cave turned out to be such a major deposit that we didn't need to go anywhere else for two solid weeks. Everything stayed nice and peaceful, and even the weather failed to bother us for the most part other than coating us in mist. The fog seemed to recede at night, and I was taken in by the beautiful clear skies full of stars.

Then one day, as our food supplies were starting to dwindle, I awoke to find both of my companions missing from camp. There were the makings of breakfast near the embers of a fire, but there was no trace of either of them. I called out for them, but only the noisy birds answered from the trees. I made sure my knife was on my belt, grabbed my pick, and then headed toward our mining site.

As I neared our mine, hidden and separated from the camp by thick trees, I heard hushed voices. Stopping in my tracks, I became aware that I'd been making crunching noises on the fallen pine needles and undergrowth. I listened, wondering what they could be talking about. I couldn't make out any words clearly, so I proceeded nearer with some trepidation. I walked such that I made as little noise as possible.

I could nearly see the clearing that held our silver deposit, and I hid behind a tree. There were Pete and Wiley, talking intensely to each other. Maybe it was my imagination, but they looked furious. The two of them were speaking in suppressed but spirited tones. Their eyes cast around every now and again.

"…I will be *damned* if I allow you to conspire behind my back," Pete was saying. I couldn't make out Wiley's response to that.

"You'll be sorry if you do!" Pete said, raising his voice somewhat. He stormed off back in the general direction of the camp and walked past me without noticing I was there.

I waited for a second, and then stepped out from behind the tree. Wiley was still near the silver deposit, staring down and deep in thought.

"What was that about?" I asked softly, and he jumped at hearing me.

"Nothing," he muttered, turning to look at the above ground mine. "Let's get to work."

I hesitated. My prospector companions hadn't been outwardly aggressive toward me, but the fear and animosity that ran under the surface of both of them made my skin crawl in discomfort.

Regardless, I got to work for the moment. It was hard to ignore the half-rotted corpse of a pickaxe lying in the dirt nearby, abandoned long ago perhaps by someone also in the midst of trouble amongst their party. I was hatching up ideas in my head;

I thought of how I could make an excuse to take my share of silver back to town and then either take a break or head out completely. In the days since we got here, we'd now mined probably a few hundred ounces of pure ore, which seemed like enough for me. The trick was going to be how I'd pitch the idea to my increasingly aloof companions.

Clouds were piling up over the mountains while the day wore on, and I grew worried about taking off right then. It took us a good day of hiking to reach the spot we were in, and I could only imagine how easy it'd be to get lost or hurt while trekking in the middle of the night, and possibly during a storm. Besides, it felt like I could break the news of my plan more easily in the morning, when perhaps Pete and Wiley would be in better spirits. It wasn't a sure bet, but I didn't have a great alternative.

We sat quietly around the campfire during supper, and the tension was as thick as ever. I tried in vain to offer some friendly conversation, hoping to brighten their moods before we all retired to sleep. It didn't work, of course. We finished in due time and left for our tents. As I retired, I wondered if the animosity had anything to do with the two of them being cramped into a single small space. I thought briefly of offering up my space for either of them, but something held me back.

Thunder began to roll in as the night grew older. Rain came with the storm, and I laid awake to the sounds of nature's fury. After an hour or so, though, I heard something different. It was a combination of thuds, splats, and scrapes. It didn't sound like anything I could guess at.

Cautiously, I poked my head out into the screaming wind and rain. Lightning occasionally lit the camp, but I couldn't see anything. Granted, it was hard just to keep my eyes open in the fierce downpour, and the lightning barely helped. I decided against calling out to see if anyone needed help, and visions flashed into my head of terrible creatures of the night stalking the camp.

I didn't sleep well, and as the night decayed into morning, I stepped out into a strange scene. The camp looked trashed. The storm apparently knocked down many large branches from the nearby trees and spread them around the whole site. It looked like a tornado had been through: the campfire spot was covered by a large fallen sapling, Pete and Wiley's tent looked like it had barely survived, and there were odd displacements of earth all over.

I glanced around, hoping for some trace of either of them. Remembering their conversation the day before, I made for the mining site. I treaded carefully, unsure what kind of mood they'd be in if I found them there again. If nothing else, I knew I'd rather see them before they could see me.

As I stepped through the trees, no voices drifted from ahead. The forest was quiet, as even the chirping birds had fallen silent. After another minute more, I *did* finally hear something, a chipping of metal on rock. Odd, since it was clear that neither of my companions had even bothered to make breakfast first.

I approached the clearing, and the sound grew louder as I saw Pete swinging away at what looked like yet another exposed vein of silver in our little mine. He looked up at me midswing, holding the pick over his head.

"Hello there!" he called with a bright tone. He wore a huge, vacant smile that left me feeling uncomfortable. I guess it was because of how dour and tense the last two weeks had been; I doubt any of us smiled during that time.

"Hi," I responded slowly. "Some storm last night."

"Yeah," Pete said jovially, resting the pickaxe on his shoulder now.

"Where's Wiley?"

The smile faded from Pete's face. He brought the pick up again and swung it down with mighty force, knocking a huge section of rock away. "Don't suspect I know," he said, raising the pickaxe again. "Run off, maybe."

I raised my eyebrows without meaning to. "Maybe," I replied, eyeing him critically. As he bent over with another large swing, his shirt flapped to the side. I stared, dumbstruck. For just a second, part of his bare chest revealed to me a mark below his neck. A gripping hand mark, black and obvious against the skin.

A chill ran the length of my spine. I had no further desire to be in his presence, so I returned to the camp with haste. I started gathering up my belongings and looked at my share of silver in the corner of my tent. It was time to leave, wasn't it? I had dismissed trouble up to now, but a missing member of our team and a disconnected reaction from the other made me recall David's words once more: *Don't get greedy. Leave at the first sign of trouble.* I wasn't sure what was going on, but it certainly qualified as trouble.

As I shut my suitcase after piling my treasure within, I thought of the other tent. A nasty thought came to me and told me I should take part of Wiley's share. He was gone, either left or dead. He wouldn't need it.

Before I could consider how stupid that was, I had already taken a couple steps with my suitcase toward the other tent. Something caught my eye that made me pause, though.

The odd displacements of mud in camp had initially defied explanation, but one particular trail of disturbance suddenly looked an awful lot to me like drag marks. I followed the trail with my eyes, and saw it head in the direction of the cave.

Dread washed over me like a bucket of cold water. Making sure I had my knife at the ready on my belt, I walked along the marks, glancing around myself at regular intervals. As I suspected, it was leading me straight to the dark cave entrance. In fact, the trail only disappeared as it crossed the threshold to the stone floor.

I froze. What would I find if I went in there? I knew without really needing to think it. Good sense demanded I turn right then and flee from that place, away from the mountains and back to the safety of Spiral Sky below. I had what I wanted, at least part of it.

I hesitated, though. I'm not even sure why; I had no obligation to Wiley. Was it just that I needed to know? I could report what happened to the sheriff if I saw it with my own eyes. Then there was the cave itself; something down there seemed to cause a chilling change in both of my companions, both mentally and perhaps physically in those mysterious marks. Or maybe I was overanalyzing things; there very well could be nothing inside. Or there could be an even larger pile of silver that the two of them didn't want me to know about.

I dropped my suitcase on the ground and crossed into the mouth of the cave and the darkness within. I had little option for light, so I decided I wouldn't go far. I moved carefully on the uneven floor, listening for any sound other than my own echoing footfalls. The daylight grew dimmer by the step, but as that happened I saw a change in the blackness. In fact, there was light within that I couldn't see before. Soft, orange light flicked at me from much deeper.

I crept further and further down into the abyss, glancing behind me every time I heard anything. I don't know how long I walked, but it had to have been a few minutes. I neared the source of the light to find an oil lamp lit and attached to the wall. I could see around the corner that another lamp was just fifty feet away, lighting the cave. There was some kind of operation in here, and it was going on right now. Nothing else would explain why the lanterns were lit and burning. I walked on slowly, snatching my head around at slight noises. I was alone, and I couldn't tell whether I'd rather it stayed that way.

Occasional passages went off in random directions, but I stuck with the largest path, as it seemed safer somehow. It went on forever, twisting and turning, and I started to worry if I'd mistake any of the smaller tunnels for the way out on my way back. Some of them were nearly the size of mine, and one was larger. I looked down after I tripped on something and saw to my shock I couldn't see the floor. There was dense, thick, rolling fog completely obscuring the area beneath my shins. It had to be a foot and half high, and there was a strict divide where it met the air. I had had enough of whatever that was, and I was ready to leave. As I prepared to turn around, I saw something sticking out of a side cavern nearby. In the dense fog, it wasn't clear what that thing was other than it was unnatural. Against my own better judgment, I stepped toward it.

As the fog swirled in my wake, the object was revealed to be a pair of boots. When I took another step, I saw the legs still attached to them. There was Wiley, lying awkwardly on his back and staring lifelessly up at the cave ceiling. I shuddered. That was what I had been afraid to find, but now I knew. I had to leave and flee this place without delay.

Something jostled a rock behind me. I spun on the spot to find Pete staring at me from twenty feet up the passage or so. He still had his pick, resting on his shoulder as he glared at me. He held our spare lantern in his other hand.

"I knew the two of you were working together," he said in a

low voice.

"Did you do this?" I asked, knowing the answer already.

"I knew it was too tempting for you heathens," Pete said in an angry tone. "We had to leave it alone. I knew Wiley tried to make a deal. But I hoped you had better sense."

"What the hell are you talking about?" I asked, my voice shaking. He was blocking the way I came in from, and the only other means of egress was to run farther into the cave.

"That *thing*," he spat, bringing the pickaxe down to rest at his side. "is a demon. Might be Lucifer himself. I won't allow you to negotiate with it. You shouldn'ta tried, 'less you wanted to end up like Wiley."

"I have no idea what you're talking about," I protested. "I'm leaving. You can have the silver. I don't want anything to do with whatever's down here."

"You *lie*," Pete snarled. "I seen you and Wiley talk during that storm. You was trying to work with it behind my back. Try to claim the awful power."

"Pete," I said, raising my hands peaceably. "I'm not working with anything or anyone. I just want to leave."

"Ain't happenin'," he said, and started to slowly move towards me. His eyes glinted in the dim lantern light. "I know what you was trying to do."

He lifted the pick as he took his next step, and I took off. I nearly tripped over Wiley as I ran into the depths of the cave, and I heard Pete hot on my tail. He was slightly slower than me, and I sprinted at full tilt into the blackness before me. I couldn't help bumping off the walls in the flickering light at my absolute sprint. Deviating from the main path seemed like a great way to get me lost, but I did so in the hope that I could lose my pursuer. I could still hear Pete's footsteps somewhere behind, but it was impossible to tell how far. I paid for glancing behind me by slamming the side of my head into something. I fell to the floor, temporarily blinded by the pain and stars flashing in my eyes. I scrambled to my feet, and saw the low hanging rock nearby, with what I could've sworn was a small bloodstain on it as something warm trickled down my forehead. I took off, but at a slower pace, stumbling off the walls as my vision slowly recovered, and I heard loud footsteps coming from somewhere. In a panic, I tried to sprint off again and ran into a narrowing tunnel wall, only to realize the steps were my own.

I stopped to catch my breath and recover my senses. It was growing colder and moister the deeper I got, and I couldn't hear footfalls behind me any longer. That was only half the battle, though. I now had to find a way out, and I knew I was hopelessly lost. I walked on, listening carefully for any sound, any sign that Pete was getting near again. I rounded a corner and found myself in total blackness. The temperature dropped nearly to freezing in an instant, and I realized as goosebumps erupted all over me that this was where the lanterns ended. I couldn't bear the thought of turning back, in case I ran into Pete in my weakened state. I'd be killed, just like Wiley.

I took a tentative step forward, and my foot crunched something that sounded like glass. Feeling desperately in my pockets, I sighed in relief to find I had a book of matches on me. With shaky, uncoordinated hands I tried and failed to strike a match, instead breaking it in half.

"Damn it!" I muttered and tried again. This time I was able to steady myself enough to find the strike strip with the head. Cradling the flame, I glanced down to see a glint of light that reflected off what I realized in a second was a broken lantern under my foot. Realizing in the back of my mind that it must've been the lost lantern from weeks prior, I picked my head up to look forward.

A dark figure stood directly in front of and just feet away from me. My breath caught in my throat, and I nearly dropped my match as the flame crawled down the stick. It wasn't Pete, though. Even illuminated, it was pure black, with a strange fuzzy edge to it like I was seeing it through watery eyes. It looked like a man, but there was no doubt that its featureless body was anything but human. I could kind-of see through it and saw that there was a giant chasm in the floor just behind it. I couldn't see how far down it went.

I couldn't breathe; I was rooted trembling to the spot. The match in my shaking hand threw strangely inconsistent light all over the cave, and illuminated the black shape before me. The thing just stood facing me, silent and still. Misery gripped at my heart, like the thing reached into me and was pulling my soul out through my stomach. I gasped, and heard for the first time in several tense seconds the beating of footsteps coming in my direction.

Something about that snapped me to my senses, though I knew Pete was no longer the primary threat to my life. Regardless, I glanced to the left to see there was another passage around the side of this cavern, and I saw lanterns lighting it. The match blew out instantly as I sprinted as fast as I could toward it and away from the shimmering figure. As I reached the lit passage, I looked back out of instinct, and my heart jumped into my throat as I saw it raise an arm to point at me. It flew toward me at unbelievable speed, and its legs remained perfectly still as it glided soundlessly over the rough stone floor. Its hand stretched out at me, aiming for my chest. I let loose a yell of fright that I've never made before, and sprinted just as hard as I could, not caring where I ended up.

I lost track of time the moment I ran from that dark chamber. I heard sounds from all directions, but I couldn't tell what they were. One minute it sounded like a howling scream, the next like thunder rolling around the stone maze. I took random turns, hoping to God that I eventually found something familiar, but I nearly stopped in my tracks when I realized I might be heading back toward the dark chasm. Paying special attention and working my memory, I tried to follow the course that best looked like where I had come from. After an eternity, I turned a corner to have daylight blast my helpless eyes. *Yes!* I sprinted with every ounce of energy I had out into the joyous sun. I didn't stop as I crossed the threshold, though. I didn't even head back to camp for my things. I just sprinted as hard as I could down the mountain, back in the direction I thought I would find the town.

As it happened, I guessed well. I suppose my survival instincts led me to the place I knew'd be safe. That was the end of the good news, though. I flagged down the first person I saw and tried my hardest to impress upon him what had happened. The man I stopped just looked at me in disgust and wouldn't even hear me. He fled from me, and I saw him eyeing me as I stood helplessly in the street. I tried to talk to several more people, but the reactions were more of the same. The looks I got ranged from fear to anger, and nobody would speak to me. I realize I must've sounded crazy, but people had died up on the mountain because of whatever that thing was. I had to tell someone.

Someone grabbed me by the shoulders and tried to steer me to the side. I whirled on the spot to find myself face to face with David, and my heart leapt with joy.

"David!" I said. "Thank God! Something terrible happened up there. There's some kind of demon creature in the cave! I think Pete and Wiley are both dead."

"Listen," he said sharply in a hushed tone. "You need to quiet down right now, and come with me."

He led me down a small alley between two buildings. I

couldn't see much of the street.

"You can't go around saying stuff like that around here," he said quietly with urgent conviction. "They won't like it."

"I don't care," I responded, not bothering to keep my voice down. "There's a demon up there, and it consumed the minds of two men. It killed them. What with all the equipment left up there, I think it's gotten others, too!"

He shushed me in a panic. "Don't you understand? *They know*." He looked horrified, as if he was just realizing it. "The people here, they have a deal with it. They keep convincing people to go up there. If they hear you talking about it, they'll kill you to keep it secret."

I eyed him with incredulity. "You can't be serious! Why would they send people to their deaths up there?"

"You're not very bright, are you? Where do you think the silver goes that gets mined? It wasn't laying around up there, right?"

I looked at him in horror. "You mean—?"

"They're complicit," he said. "And I guess I am too. I've benefitted from it, even though I was just born into it. I'm sorry for ever telling you to go up there, but if you want to live, you need to quietly leave right now and never return."

I shook my head. "This is sick. I'm not going anywhere. I'm going to see that thing destroyed and banished from this world. It's wrong what's going on here." I left him there without another word. I had a small amount of money in my pocket, and

I stepped into the saloon to rent a room for the night after downing a whiskey in one awful gulp.

And that's where I am now. I decided as soon as I came up here to write down what happened to me, because I intend to put a stop to this madness. Men aren't made to suffer demons walking the Earth among them, and if I can't destroy it, I can at least trap it. I'm going to use the last of my money to buy as much dynamite as I can, and I'm going to blow the entrance to the cave. Then at least I can stop anyone else falling into what I now know to be a deliberate trap. I wouldn't be surprised if the silver itself was made by that monster to lure people in. Once I trap it, I'm going to take all the silver we mined and I'm heading out of here. I hope to never hear the words "Spiral Sky" again.

There's someone banging on the door. I'll

Nicole Godfrey

Nicole Godfrey is a writer who calls beautiful Colorado home, along with her furry children. She was born in Omaha, Nebraska and has lived in Florida and Tennessee. Her writing started with poetry, leading to her first publication at the age of twelve. She has three short stories published through Colorado Springs Fiction Writers Group: "A Page Lost" in *An Uncommon Collection*, "The Power of the Word" in *Remnants and Resolutions: Tales of Survival*, and "Trials of the Moon" in *Colorado State of Mind*. Her full-length, co-authored titles include *Hoofbeats, Chasing the Waves,* and *Open Skies* with AJ Marcus. Nicole actively participates in Amtgard, loves to play table-top RPGs, dabbles in all forms of artwork, and attends college at PPCC.

They All Fall Down

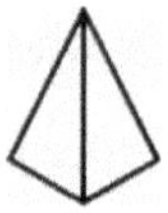

Young Adult Magical Realism

by

Nicole Godfrey

I walk the halls of this school every day, just like I've walked the halls of so many others before. I don't want to be here. Or at least, I don't want to want to be here, but these people fascinate me so. Like that girl there. Pale blonde hair glistening in the fluorescent light, perfect smile plastered on her face, brand new clothes from the top of her perfectly groomed head to the tips of her designer shoes, and the detail in carefully applied make-up. Kids flock around her, complimenting her, laughing with her, eager for attention, and yet none of them see how hollow she is.

But I do.

As usual, not one of them notices me. I like it that way. The unobserved observer. Indulging in my curious obsession and not having to explain myself. What a thrill it gives me, an unending flow of pure adrenaline that makes me vibrate as I walk with soundless steps. This is my hunting ground, and all of them, my unwilling prey.

I prefer the hurried moments between to the classes themselves, with their overly repeated knowledge and biased opinions that no one but a captive audience will listen to. The old are not as exciting as the young, the ones who still see all the potential in their short lives. But I sit through the classes anyways, something fun always happens one way or another.

They could see me, if they wanted to, the young ones. All they have to do is pay attention when a shadow passes through their peripheral vision. But most of them can't get around the narrow scope encompassing their world. That comes with time. And time is what makes them forget their deep-seated wonder. So, none of them see me.

That's why I don't want to be here. If not for the intrigue I find in watching, I think I'd give up. Therein lies the true problem. Giving up means the burning would start. And I ask you, how is one supposed to indulge in watching if the whole world is burning? You can't, so giving up isn't an option.

A fight breaks out in the hallway.

It's not surprising to me, but it amuses. I watch two boys throw punches while rolling around on the floor. One lands a good hit, opening a cut over the other boy's eye and causing him to stagger back. The one who landed the hit takes advantage and slams his rival against the ground. The impact is enough to knock the boy out cold with a loud CRACK.

A small smile tugs at my lips and I look up to assess the reactions from the audience. They're shocked, for the most part, but a few cheer for the victor as he's pulled to his feet by a security guard. Teachers flock in to tend to the unconscious boy.

A single gaze strays from the spectacle. The eyes behind that gaze are locked on the area I occupy. I look closer. Yes, there's a boy staring in my direction.

I glance around, but there is no one else standing close to me. I'm tucked away in a corner, having backed up during the fray.

A Paramedic wheels a stretcher into the dispersing crowd. He assists one of the teachers in putting the injured boy on the collapsible bed before strapping him down. The teachers wave off the remaining onlookers. But behind them, the only one willing to stick around, stands the boy. His dark hair falls across a furrowed brow and covers most of his right eye. Dark grays make up his outfit, his arms cross in a tight self-embrace, and a hip bag hangs from his shoulder.

As a test, I move to my right, and I can't hide my smile when his eyes follow me. So there is one who sees beyond. My curiosity peaks to find out why he's different. No time like the present. The smoky shadows, which are my constant companions, swirl around my legs as I walk deeper into the building.

I don't have to look back, he's following me, and I can feel it. Like a tingle of awareness at the back of my mind. Dark and secluded, that's my goal, and what better place than the library?

As I walk down the rows, my fingers trail over the spines of books that line the shelves. A dying art some say, but I don't agree. Books will always have their place, even in a world suffocated by technology, such as the current state of reality.

My back rests against the far wall when he catches up to me. He stops, half surprised to see me waiting for him. He swallows hard, his throat working reflexively, and then he recoups. His arms cross back over his chest and he leans against the pillar opposite me.

"Who are you?" His voice is pleasant and melodic.

"Do you really want to know?" My voice grates in contrast, the lack of use making me sound guttural and forbidding.

"I wouldn't be here if I didn't." He moves his hair out of his face, looking me up and down.

I know what he sees, whether he believes it or not is another matter. Ashen skin with dark tipped fingers. Hair braided intricately around a small set of horns. Steel gray eyes as cold as the grave. And then there are my wings. A pair of sweeping shadows that look to be in constant motion.

"If you insist. I'm a companion of Death, cousin of the Fates, and the eternal Lost Soul." I stop, leaving him to absorb what I've said.

"That's all very well and good, but what's your name?" He seems to be amused at this, as if the words I speak are just a flight of fancy, and a handsome smile lights up his face.

I smile in turn. "You may call me Phaedra."

"That's a very unusual name." But he smiles wider all the same.

"I know, but it fits me." I twirl my finger and wrap a shadow around it, gathering energy to me.

"So, why are you here? I can tell you're not...human." The idea excites him. I see it plain as day in the expression on his face.

"I walk unseen, hidden by the shadows of obscurity. I'm only seen by those who are ready. Because it's always the same. For all of you eventually. Ashes to ashes, they all fall down." I step forward, closing the gap between us, and cup his face in my cold hands. With a kiss on his lips we vanish. Nobody is left for those who mourn. No explanation.

Time to find another school.

Stan Griffin

Stanley D. Griffin, born in Lubbock Texas, enlisted in the U.S. Army right out of high school. His first duty assignment—Ft. Carson, Colorado. He fell in love twice during that time; first, with his loving wife Patricia; and second, with the Colorado mountains. He came back to Colorado Springs after a long career in the Army. He joined Colorado Springs Fiction Writers Group in 2009. Stanley has written several unpublished novels including: *The Treachery of Zethus*, *A World Away* and his current works in the Lucius Balder series, *Fortunate Meeting*, *Body Pirates*, and *Home Coming*. He has also written a few novelettes: *Oracle Lake*, *The Last James*, *Eons of Numbness*, and two published short stories, "A Deep Gaming Experience" in the *A Colorado State of Mind* anthology and the dark science fiction "Sedna 90377" in this anthology.

Sedna 90377

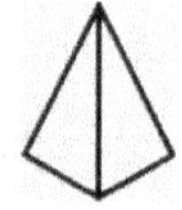

Dark Science Fiction

by

Stanley Griffin

My mind cleared as I regained consciousness. I recognized the slight rhythmic bouncing. I was in a tube shuttle. Rapid vibrations meant it was moving fast. I opened my eyes and all I saw was blackness. I strained to move, but I was held to a gurney by a full body restraining field. "Damn it!" The only thing I could move was my mouth, so I shouted once more. "What the hell is going on? Where am I?"

"So, you're awake finally," a feminine voice remarked. Lights came up slowly but stayed dim, just bright enough that I could see the ceiling and part of the stark interior of the shuttle. More of a round tube with an airlock at one end. Even though the gurney was tilted slightly up, I couldn't see myself.

"Who are you?" I shouted. As I fought against the field holding me. "Where are you, and where the hell am I?" A sudden glow appeared in the shuttle near the foot of the gurney. It wavered with static for a second, then coalesced into a hologram. A tall and very attractive woman with long black hair appeared. All I could do was look past my nose at her. Slowly, she stepped closer. She dragged her holographic finger down the edge of the bed as she walked the few steps to my right side. Dressed in a tight, strapless, black leather dress, she looked smoking hot. Things I'd love to do to her rolled through my mind. *I want to get her out of that leather.* "Hey sexy, where am I?"

"You're in a tube shuttle traveling a quarter mile under the ice from the space port complex, on your way to cell block five," she replied.

"And you're a hologram, right?"

"Yes, I am, Timothy," she replied, her voice smooth and soft as honey. "At least what you're seeing is. I'm real enough, I'm just not in the shuttle with you."

I gave her my best smile. "Do you think that I'm that dangerous? I can't even touch you."

She shrugged her bare shoulders. "No, why?"

"Do you think a restraining field is necessary, darling."

"We've found over the years that it's better to keep prisoners…" she paused and then pointed a slim finger at me, "like you, restrained. At least until your transfer into the prison airlock is complete. We've had a few try to commit suicide before they reach the cell block. It looks bad on my status reports."

"Really? Well you won't have that kind of trouble out of me."

"We'll see," she said with a smile. She clasped her hands together and added, "When you arrive, the gurney you're on will turn upright and push you into the airlock. There it will release you, so be prepared for a short drop. Make certain you remain in the airlock. Some have tried to jump back onboard the shuttle. It never works out for them. You see, this shuttle will depressurize the instant the cell block doors close. The temperature will drop to minus 300 and something degrees." She waved her hand in the air. "I never can keep trivial things like that straight. It's minus 400 and something degrees on the surface, but who cares, right? It's a security measure to prevent inmates from escaping back into the space port. That's why I'm here as a holograph, I wouldn't survive the trip back to the space port. Oh, and remember, once you're inside the airlock you'll meet the rest of your cell block. They'll get you…" she turned away and held a hand to her mouth, "settled in."

"So who the hell are you?"

She turned around with a big grin on her face. "I am Miranda Howell. I'm warden of Sedna 90377, one of nine Zeus Corporation penal facilities. And I have less than forty-five minutes to give your orientation. That's how long it takes for the tube shuttle to get from the space port to the cell blocks."

"But I'm innocent," I shouted. "I was framed!"

Miranda rolled her eyes. "I have an entire prison full of men who swear they're innocent. And just like you, I don't believe any of them."

She briefly raised a finger. "Back to your orientation. The first thing I have to give you is a short history lesson. This iceberg was named after a vengeful sea goddess named Sedna. Sedna 90377 is a dwarf planet discovered on November 14th, 2003. It is a trans-Neptunian object that takes approximately 11,400 Earth years or so to complete an orbit of the Sun."

"And I need to know this why?" I argued.

She looked at me like she had caught me staring at her breasts. After a second, she continued, "It's part of the orientation, don't worry, there won't be a test." She stared at me for a moment. "The Hartman Corporation mined this planet for methane and other minerals starting in 2978. The company went bankrupt and abandoned Sedna. The Zeus Corporation acquired Sedna in 3055 and transformed the mines into a corporate prison."

"Fuck the Zeus Corporation, I hate it! It calls itself a corporation. But really it's just as corrupt a government as the one on Earth!"

"Yes," Miranda scowled. "Watch your language." She paused then continued. "For the last two and a half centuries, Zeus Corporation has been setting up mining operations, research facilities, colonies, and shipyards throughout the solar system. Now more people have worked for Zeus enterprises throughout the solar system than live on planet Earth. That's why the Zeus Corporation became its own government complete with laws and penal codes. Therefore, it was a simple transition into operating its own prisons. You should be aware that as such, this facility does not fall under Earth penal laws. So we have a much broader scope of punishments we can use to reform inmates."

She reached out and her arm disappeared when it exited the hologram beam. When it reappeared, she held a data board. "It says you are Timothy Maynard, and you have quite a rap sheet. Back on Earth you committed everything from data hacking, armed robbery, to assault with a deadly weapon."

"And I spent my time in prison for those charges!" I raged.

"Why, yes, that's true." She nodded. "But that was back on Earth before you took employment with Zeus Corp. You did relatively well for a few years according to this report, but you started to use recreational pharmaceuticals. That's when you went back to being not so good a citizen. Now you're convicted on five counts of serial rape. That's why you've gotten yourself placed in my facility."

"Like I said, I was framed," I argued. "All of those women wanted it that way. I was just role playing with them. They wanted to play the helpless lady caught by a bad man. There's a lot of women like that out there, you know. They have a need for that kind of shit. It's just afterwards they made up lies about me."

"I still don't believe you," Miranda replied matter of fact. "You've been sentenced to five consecutive eleven-year sentences. That's Earth years, by the way. You'll be glad to know, that's 360 days to a year. Twenty-four hours to a day. We don't do a leap year out here. That's a total of fifty-five years to your sentence. But if you're on your best behavior, you might only see thirty-five of that."

She took a step closer and looked down at me as if she saw something she liked. *Maybe I can play this bitch. Get on her good side. If I can get the warden as a pet, I'd be set.* "Well, if I have to be in prison, this is going to be the best one yet."

She laughed. "And why is that?"

"You're the sexiest warden I've ever had." I winked. "Why don't you make me your personal office boy? I can clean and polish up everything, including you."

Her eyes went wide, and she licked her lower lip. Then her nostrils flared, and a mischievous smile grew that gave her an evil look.

It kinda made me nervous.

"I might just do that," she said. "Do you have any idea why a woman would be the warden of an all-male penitentiary housing the very worst offenders?"

"I have no clue. Maybe you just like knowing all the men in this place dream about you in their bunks at night? By the way, I also do great back and foot rubs."

Her hologram wavered with static as she bent down close to

my face. "It would likely be, because I do not like men as sexual partners, ever. I had a bad experience a long time ago that changed my attitude about men."

"Maybe I can help change you back, Warden Miranda Howell. Just give me a chance." I gave her my best I-want-you smile. *I must be getting to her. I see the tiniest hint of hard nipples pressing against her tight leather dress. Ohhh, I may have this bitch in my pocket.*

"We'll see," she said. With that same almost evil smile, Miranda straightened. "But you can call me Mistress Miranda. All of my…" she paused, "friends do. I just might invite you to my quarters some night for a few games. I doubt you'll like it as much as I do. But for now, we need to finish your orientation."

She pointed to my other side as another woman appeared in hologram form.

Oh my god! She was tall, slim, with shoulder length brown hair, brown eyes, and perfect breasts. She smiled at Miranda. In her hand she had a data board. *What luck, two drop dead gorgeous women. If I can't get to the warden, maybe I can make time with her. That would work well for me, yeah.*

"I want you to meet this facility's chief doctor, Doctor Leda Swan. Our good doctor trained with the solar system's premier doctor in full body modifications. You might have heard of him, Doctor Willard Sharman."

"Isn't he the guy that's been making people into animal hybrids? You know human-like cats, dogs, birds, and reptiles and such," I replied.

"Why, yes, he is," Miranda replied. "He's also known for his breakthroughs in transgender body modification as well. But for now, Doctor Leda will tell you about the body modifications she has done to you, so that you can survive on Sedna 90377."

My heart raced, and a cold knot grew in my stomach. "What the Fuck! What the hell have you done to me?" Beads of sweat started to cover my forehead along with a wave of nausea that sent the taste of bile to my mouth.

"First, I have injected you with a mass of Nanorobotic cells," the doc replied smoothly.

"You mean nanites?" I asked.

She looked at me as if she would love to drill a hole right through my head.

"Yes, nanites."

A chill ran up my spine.

Doctor Swan read from her data board once more, "This is to help keep you healthy while you stay here in our facility. The nanites have attached themselves to your bones and are now emitting a low level negative magnetic charge. This charge is minuscule by itself. But with the mass of nanites inside you, combined with the facility's floor giving off a positive magnetic charge, this helps to simulate one Earth gravity. It's due to the low gravity on Sedna 90377 that we have to do this. However, you will be required to exercise twice a day to stay healthy."

"I don't do exercise," I rebuffed.

"We have ways of giving you an incentive to stay fit," Miranda said.

Doctor Swan stayed silent until Miranda said, "Continue, Doctor."

"Twice a day you will be required to work out in either the heavy gravity obstacle room or on our incline running track," said Doctor Swan. "You'll like the heavy gravity obstacle room or the HGO as we call it. We bump up the floor's positive magnetic charge to simulate higher than one Earth gravity. You will then climb over, through, and around padded obstacles at one and a half simulated Earth gravity. Then you'll graduate to two, then two and a half times Earth's gravity. If you can handle it, we'll push you to three times Earth's gravity. No one has ever managed to go beyond three."

"And if I just sit on my ass?" I asked.

"You won't," Miranda replied. "Continue, Leda."

"Or you will be required to run for fifteen minutes on our incline track," Leda continued. "This track is set at a thirty-two degree slant. As you run around it, your body will be subjected to the effects of centrifugal force, as well as a simulated higher than Earth gravity. This load on your body twice a day will help prevent muscle and bone atrophy."

"I only do one kind of exercise," I joked. "And it requires a partner of the opposite sex."

Miranda laughed hard. "That's great, that's precisely the incentive we use. We place three inmates or guards in the room with you. Even my guards need an incentive for exercise. If you can stay away from them and not get caught, you get to go back to the cell block and brag. But if you get caught," Miranda gave her evil grin once more, "the rule is, if they catch you, they can have you."

"Oh hell no!" I yelled.

"You've been in prison before." Miranda smirked. "You know that sort of thing happens. We just use it as an incentive for you to be compliant."

"You can't do that!" I yelled. "It's against the law." My heart pounded in my chest.

"On Earth, yes, you're right. But this is a corporate penitentiary, governed by corporate laws. While it is a necessary part of business, this facility does not add to the corporate bottom line. So I have full reign to make sure you don't enjoy your stay here. That's also what happens when you piss off one of the corporate heads by raping her daughter. Dumb ass," Miranda stabbed a finger at me.

Miranda smiled wide and leaned close once more. "My supervisors never come out here to inspect the facility. They look at the place over closed circuit cameras placed all around the detention center. We then teleconference once a month over what they've seen."

My heart beat like a directional thruster gone rogue. I couldn't believe they were allowed to use such treatment. Stunned, I stared back at her slack jawed.

Miranda stood and said, "By the way, your prison jump suits are held closed with Hrayek tear away fasteners. You know the stuff that doesn't have the hard backing. That stuff always cuts and chafes so much. It's more expensive, but it's worth it."

She touched the base of my throat. "They start here at your neck." She traced a line down my upper body with her finger. "Then go all the way down past your crotch." She stopped at my crotch, then came back up to my waist. "And back around to your waist. I designed the uniform myself, by the way." She waved her hand dismissively at me. "No, you don't have to thank me. I just don't want anyone to hang themselves with a belt or draw string. You'll find the inmates like the ease of getting in and out of them as well. You don't even need to strip past your waist to go to the bathroom. Just rip open the seams in the right places and sit down."

The tube shuttle decelerated. Miranda pointed to the airlock. "You're almost there. Are you ready to meet your new cell mates?"

The gurney tilted forward and the lights got brighter. The field that held my head went away and I looked around. Seeing more of the shuttle. I noticed full length mirrors framing the airlock door. Looking in the mirrors, I saw a woman with short blonde hair, nice tits, and fair figure reflected back at me. I moved my head back and forth to make sure it was me. I was dressed in a pink jumpsuit and pink slip-on prison shoes, for God's sake. Shaken by the sight I screamed, "What the fuck did you do to me?" I struggled against the retaining field. Sweat streamed down my face as my heart tried to beat its way out of my chest.

"I told you, our good Doctor was expertly trained to be one of the best in body modification. She has given you a whole new outlook on life. You see, most inmates don't like child molesters or rapists. At first, they didn't tend to survive long in my prison. So now I have Leda change every rapist or molester into a woman." She played with my hair. "Like you. Then, we place you in general population. When a rapist leaves my reformatory, they are truly reformed. They never again feel the need to force themselves on another woman, ever."

"Bitches, you turned me into a woman!" I screamed.

"No need to be mean," Miranda objected, as she gave me a malevolent smile that faded quickly.

"You know that you can't put a female in a male prison!" I shouted

"But remember..." Miranda's smile appeared again.

I hated that look of hers.

"All the documentation transferring you here says you're male." She pointed to her data board. "You were male when you got off the transfer ship. And you'll be male again when you get back on it to leave." Her eyes flashed wide once more. "Just think, in moments you're going to be the most popular girl in cell block five." She laughed. "I mean, you're going to make friends very quickly, I'm sure."

In stunned silence I stared at myself in the mirrors while Miranda talked.

"I'll give you a few months to… you know, get to know your new friends. Then I'll call you to my personal dungeon beneath my quarters. There Leda and I can have a little private play time with you." Her eyes flashed wildly. "Bitch! It's going to be so much fun. For us anyway. You see, you'll come to us bound and helpless. And my sweetness," she touched her finger to my nose, "we'll keep you that way, I promise. Like I told you before, I…" she looked at Leda then finished, "we only like women. And since you're now female, Leda and I want to play with you as often as we can. We've a way with making pain feel wonderful. Oh, do you still want to be my little office bitch? I can still arrange that for you."

I could only stare at my reflection.

Doctor Swan said, "You're not going to like it in general population so you might as well learn to live with it. You're going to find out just what it's like to be forced into having sex. Over and over you'll experience it for the rest of your time here. If you're lucky, you'll get turned into some inmate's bitch. You might even get married to one of them. Then he'll prostitute you out to the others for things he wants. Good thing about that is you'll have some protection from getting taken in the middle of the night. You see, from time to time we leave certain cell doors unlocked. It helps keep up morale among the inmates."

Miranda added, "It's used to maintain compliance, you see.

If inmates are very good, they'll get rewarded with a night with you. So long as they're back in their cells by morning roll call, I'm good with whatever they do to you. They're not allowed to kill you that is. I can't have that. I give them what they want, and they are nice and refrain from being disruptive. That keeps my bottom line low and my bosses like it. So everybody wins." Miranda tapped her chin with her finger. "Everybody wins, but you. Damn. Sucks to be you. Don't worry, you're one of sixteen we have in cell block five. However, you'll be quite busy for a while. Being the new girl and all."

Leda reached out and touched my crotch. "Don't worry about your missing parts, I have them on ice for you. When you get ready for parole, I'll put them back where they belong good as new. It's easy to do, you know. But while you're here, you won't need them."

She stroked the side of my face with her hand, then flicked the end of my nose with her finger. "Oh, and by the way, I made you physically unable to have an orgasm. Wouldn't want you learning to enjoy this, you know. You'll experience everything it is to be a woman. You'll even have a monthly cycle. Oh, but you won't get pregnant. We can't have that in an all-male facility, now can we? Requesting diapers in our supply runs would be embarrassing."

The shuttle banged to a stop. "God damn it!" I felt myself getting faint. The airlock doors opened one at a time. Then the gurney moved towards the narrow portal. Miranda and Leda laughed as I moved my head side to side as I fought to escape the restraining field.

"By the way, Timothy, we've changed your name. For the time you're here you'll be known as Tabatha." They both laughed wildly as the gurney pushed me the rest of the way into the airlock.

"You fucking evil cunts!" I screamed.

Pain shot through my hands and knees when the restraining field shut off, and I hit the floor. I heard muffled shouts of men from outside the inner airlock doors. I looked back and the gurney blocked the entire doorway. As I was getting to my feet the outer airlock door closed with a loud bang. I looked out one of the small windows in the double doors and watched the gurney retracting as the shuttle moved away, its back airlock door wide open to the vacuum of space. Miranda and Leda moved into the shuttle doorway. They just waved and smiled as it sped away.

I looked quickly around the eight foot by eight foot room. Then, the inner airlock doors opened. Several men ran into the space. Shouts, grunts, whistles, and footfalls of the men fighting their way into the airlock overwhelmed me. Before I could move, several hands grabbed me roughly, spun me around, and pinned me to the outer door. My arms were jerked behind my back. I couldn't break free. Many hands grabbed and groped at me, refusing to let me get away. Several inmates dragged me into the hallway and down the corridor passed cells to the main common room. Several different smells assaulted me, body odor mixed with sweat, vomit, piss, trash, and shit wafted around me. Without warning, I was shoved over a table. My face impacted the steel tabletop leaving the taste of blood in my mouth. Pain shot through my breasts from being pressed hard against the table. The smell of disinfectant overtook the smell of BO. Someone grabbed my arms and pulled them over my head. I forced my face up, my chin pressed hard into the table. A throng of men crowded the other side of the table. A large man dropped to a squat in front of me. Several dark prison tattoos covered his face. He smiled at me and blew me a kiss. Over the roar of shouts, cheers, and catcalls, I heard the sickening sound of many sets of Hrayek fasteners being torn apart.

Jazz Feylynn

Jazz Feylynn is a new explorer in the world of creative writing. She adds being a writer to an exciting life which includes colorful multimedia artist, photographer, needle worker, herbalist, bicyclist, movie and anime fanatic, and avid reader of many flavors. Plants and critters share her life, and she incorporates them into her stories.

Author of fantasy, paranormal, speculative fiction, creative nonfiction, and historical archiving, her life changing universes accentuate the hidden energies glimmering with beauty in a story's soul. Jazz loves to travel the world and beyond writing embellished adventures in the magical and mystical realms, communicating with angels, fairies, dragons and otherworldly beings.

Jazz Feylynn has been a member of CSFWG's wildly fun Saturday group since 2010, the Saturday officer 2015-2017, and a Pike's Peak Writers member since 2012.

Writing Bound

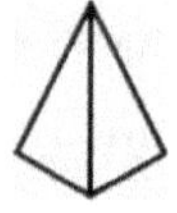

Urban Fantasy Essay

by

Jazz Feylynn

I received an e-mail at home on my laptop from my women's writing group with an assignment. The message contained a ticking—tick-tock, tick-tock—time bomb deadline.

A writing prompt that could damn well fling all the words across my face and the ink stain my hands a gory mess before I finished. That left me in a hell of a situation beyond my abilities.

My group's leader was fearless—she had to be—to have proposed such a chore: spend 20 minutes freewriting in our personal time completing her exercise. Of course, this was a means to an end for her. By adding minutes outside the monthly meeting, she doubled up our usual measly amount allotted for a writing exercise session. Real sneaky.

The writing task was not the only issue of the destructive countdown. No, the quest to find a word, one verb, was another issue which ate up the duration I needed to freewrite. Indeed, it was an extremely challenging assignment.

She added 10 minutes to what I spent every morning freewriting. Besides, there was the allotment to add additional thought retrieving said perfect verb to write about. Yep, definitely demanding, making such a request.

The verb had to be tremendous. Not mousey. Not dull. An unrestrained no-holds-barred verb that stood out among all other verbs. A single verb with an impact that could stand the long haul and not wimp out after the second hand had tick-tocked by.

I came upon an idea to go find and hassle somebody to help me figure out a verb to use. It could have been anyone. With my whitened fingers clutched to my chest, I would wail, "Please, pick a verb for me," beseeching a miracle. "Please, it's gotta be a great verb. *Please, help me!*"

It did not seem fair to burden someone else with the explosive aftermath that would come—and it would—when the deadline of one-thousand-two-hundred seconds had passed.

Unable to process the one verb to use, my mind filled with chaotic verbiage from the hundreds of possibilities spiking and looping in multiple directions throughout my head, none actually took hold. "Pick one and get it over with," I pleaded with myself. *"Pick one!"*

That word, pick, stuck in my head. Pick. Picking is a verb. I pick you. Like the horror film on the kindergarten playground of memories, of being the last one chosen, this last-ditch verb was alone and unneeded. That didn't seem like the grand verb to fill my writing time. I choked with indecision. It tasted unpleasant.

Then it came to me, the one verb that I had worked hard with over the years. It would work. I had chosen the perfect verb. It would be perfection.

An attack plan needed to be formulated. What method was I to proceed with? Plan A: the computer. Alternatively, I could go with Plan B: putting ink to paper. Plan A's drawback was the time, about 10 minutes, spent getting ready to attack the digital page: turning on the computer, opening programs, dictionaries, guides, web pages, and documents. Everything I needed to get me through my challenge trauma, to set that outstanding writing tool up and running, would eat away time for writing. Plan B, a time-honored approach handed down through the ages, sounded faster at first, getting down the words. However, I had to transfer all those written words onto the computer, which added to the time limit yet again.

I decided to go with Plan B and wield my secret weapon, the one I associated with all my freewriting: *purple ink.*

As the computer warmed up, I'd write in the comfortable old-fashioned way. Once the computer was online, I would pound the keys. I'd transfer the words I had written in that exceptional color, thereby, saving time by overlapping writing, the computer's cumbersome start up, and of all my additional needy needs.

With my worn purple ink pen and paper in hand--that I reserved for all those freewriting mornings that had come and gone, those to come--I began to write about the verbiage I had chosen in this unexpected and unasked for daunting task.

The stopwatch threat hung over me. I set the timer with shaky clammy fingers. The silent reckoning with the not-so-silent alarm blast at the end of the merciless countdown commenced.

My pen ended up on a writing tour within my mind, conducted by an adorable boy dressed in several subtle shades of blue. He, with his familiar quirky nerdy attitude, showed me the sights along my disastrous writing memory lane. The road had detours, stop signs, missed turns, hills and valleys, deep dark tangled forests, ruts and potholes, icy patches, and spinouts along the way. There were blank spots, ellipses, and even a few areas (okay, actually many, lots, a humongous amount) for—"*To Be Filled In At A Later Date.*"

As I glimpsed my stumbling failings while learning to write, this feisty youth brought me underneath a freeway overpass. The hidden speedy discourse of others brainier than I drifted down from the multilane composition highway. With each key click and scratch above, reminders echoed of the ease with which others flew through what had always been my drudgery.

The concrete structure overhead was fractured throughout. Cracks rippled down every support without exception. Hardened cement chunks languished on the ground. Gray dust particles spewed into every crevice. The wordless, like the homeless, desired this place as a sheltered haven.

Beneath the overpass, the blue boy pointed out an oversized, red, cardboard box where out popped a waif of a boy who had hidden within the flimsy, tattered, corrugated walls. He was not so cute, looking as though he had lived through a deluge of besmirched corrected papers that ended wadded up. His hair was greasy and matted with a torrent of spikes and tufts. His perky nose twitched and snatched out all flaws to the nth degree.

He was clothed in a shirt and combat pants, both red with varying flaming patterns. Some crimson lines had faded with time; some, vivid and bright, had never disintegrated from my mind. The horrid bloody admonitions hovered around me for never having been good enough with the written word. Under bright scarlet hair, teachers' favorite pigmentation of ink, the awful cast splashed and dripped down his face, a grisly reminder of mistakes that had bruised.

The delightful and cute blue boy's striking looks contrasted with the red waif. Exquisite shades of blue ebbed and flowed with creative subconscious thoughts.

"Red is his favorite color," the adorable blue boy uttered. We stared at the glare of scarlet fumes on the waif. The crimson covered him from head to toe. It was hard to find an empty space available to add more of the morose stain. "He says it's the hue of life and *death*, a vibrating life-giving glow. The tint is pumped full of oxygenated writing creativity. Words combine with the ever-widening blood puddles spilled from the suffocating death wounds."

I knew all too well the damage of red ink smeared across page-after-page offering neither encouragement nor any compliments at all. Every bloody mark had assassinated my words along the way.

The waif had a devious shine in his eyes. He reached beneath the grubby cardboard lid, moving his arm back and forth in search of something unknown. His eyes never blinked or wavered from mine, encompassing me in a controlling field. A bump and a thump, his careless hands knocked over something heavy. His eyes, if anything, gleamed even more brightly, having found the treasure he sought.

He moved ever so hastily, determined to enshroud his enchantment over me. His hands, a swirling red mass, moved from under the lid. Grasped within his palms he carried, of all things, what looked like a pencil box but not the standard kind given to children on the first day of school, that helped them through the years. This peculiar, carved, bloody box was a teacher's toolbox delight, and also a Chinese puzzle-lock box. His deft fingers worked each coded step to unlock the maze. He shifted a piece here and poked in another piece there.

Rivulets of sweat oozed down my forehead. My limbs became glued in the grimy gray underpass muck. The slushy ground persisted in sinking me ever deeper, a feeling I've had for as long as I could remember.

Swiftly he finished the intricate movements and the last piece detached with a click. It held me spellbound in suspended animation. My heart palpitated. The top slid to reveal the most precious of trade secrets.

The malicious waif plucked out a tangled red string, its strands twisted and knotted into an odd hobble. A caged deterrent, if ever there was one. This was not to constrict or bind one's physical movement. Every hobble allowed just enough room to see between the bars at life's nourishment. Anyone thus restrained, was in some kind of bondage, faltering in a limited range that constrained each within his or her own personal penitentiary, with the richness denied always in view. I assumed this yoke would encase me as well as any hobble, only this one bound the mind.

With a flick of a hand, the waif tossed the red snarled string. The flash of scarlet settled upon me. Its touch seared my mind. A noose tightened around the words, sentences, and paragraphs of communication I used. I was speechless, hands tied. It cut me off, trapped and held me within my own silent dark word tomb.

The waif smirked. "It's an age-old teaching form I practice, executing embarrassing snare methods to guide students with value and purpose." Spittle escaped his lop-sided grin. "No matter how much harm done during cruel lessons, my way to teach is **tradition**." In his derangement, snickers dribbled back to me.

Writing Bound

He went back into his sleazy dilapidated box and disappeared from view. He was hidden but never gone. A quick laugh seeped through the gaps now and then, vibrated the container. I knew no matter how much time passed, the waif's cackling influence would continue perpetually from deep within. I struggled to traverse the terrain of writing down thoughts freely and easily, forever bound by limits ingrained, not yet overcome.

The superb boy in blue turned to leave like Dickens' spirits of Christmas, his job completed. With his tour ended, I came back from the depths of thought. I blinked and took a few clearing breaths, taking a few moments to sort through all that I'd learned.

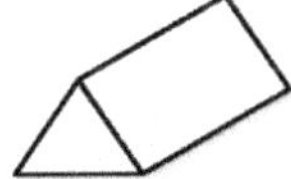

A touch of red in the ink, the life-supporting creative oxygen mixed with blue ink's solid stability, blended into a stunning purple written enlightenment. An imaginative mixture of words, thoughts, ideas, stories, and dreams that came out of my subconscious mind that never could bind the verb *writing*.

These days, it is even more critical for me to continue writing than worry about those annihilating strokes slashed across my penned heartfelt words, those old limits and blood red ink stains splashed on my black and white crisply written pages. I ignore the deranged laughter seeping out from the underpass depths of consciousness and forge ahead on my writing journey through life.

Sangita Kalarickal

A CSFWG alumna, Sangita is a fantasy writer with a soft corner for literary fiction. She lives in Minnesota with her husband, kid, and the several characters she writes about. She loves writing short stories though she is now finishing final touches to her first novel.

In the spirit of the theme for this anthology, Sangita has chosen to merge science fiction and fairy tale genres.

THE BARTER
Science Fiction Fairy Tale

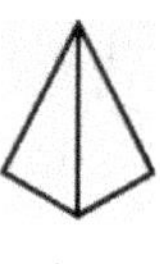

by

Sangita Kalarickal

Once upon a time, Time spun around. Things were here yet they were not. It was then, yet it was not.

Eli stepped into the mustiness of the *Gedächtniskirche* ruins and whispers of gliding cars and loud swooshes of public transport vehicles whizzed by and vanished. The broken church, as it was often called, appeared puny nestled in the sleek lines of Berlin's landscape. The remains of an era long gone, the structure stood as an oasis of calm in the midst of a hurried metropolis. Eli, soaked in the tranquility offered by the monument, waited for the ghosts of bygone times floating about the memorial hall to soothe his disturbed state. On the floor, the mosaic of Archangel Michael battling a dragon reflected the struggle in his mind.

The Barter

Twenty-one hours remained before his twenty-first birthday, exact to the minute. He dreaded this day. The day stood as a pivot in time for a chain of events set into motion exactly 400 years ago. Standing in the church at the end of the 21st century, Eli looked around and his mind whirled with the memories along with the explanations and the fantasy that underlined them all.

Even today, his heart raced as he remembered the delicate beeping of his communication device a week ago. The little white tele-visio-portal device had only put through a voice call, no visual connection.

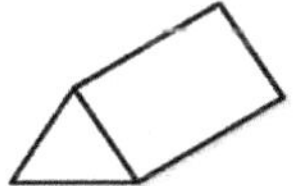

"Herr Bergmann," a metallic voice said. "Your father collapsed at his office. You may visit him at the hospital." The robot teleportal operator then related fuzzy details of the incident. Paramedics had rushed his father to the Care Center, but his vital signs were steadily deteriorating, for no apparent reason.

Eli quickly stepped out of his office glancing back to confirm the body sensor had signed him out for the day. He could not afford to lose hours at the part-time job he had managed to hold on to at Stadt Bibliothek. The city library was not the best paying employer, but it gave him access to a wonderful world of ancient history, languages and mythology, which he studied for his advanced degree. Also, Eli appreciated the value of an old-fashioned library for his research.

He had to get to the hospital. Quick. It cost him a good chunk of his monthly salary, but he simply had to teleport. No time to spare. Guilt gave him a sense of urgency as he recalled the falling out with his father. Urgency and guilt. The guilt stayed and festered.

Emo was always in his life, always in his face, always wanting to be a part of every decision. Yes, Emo was being a father, but Eli needed his independence. The stifling feeling of being dominated held his throat until Eli felt he could breathe no more. He had finally slammed the door in his father's face and walked out into uncertainty. "Uncertain future, yes, but at least it will be of my own making," he had explained to his mother later.

The falling out with his father nibbled at his conscience, especially after the hospitalization news, and fed his guilt.

Eli turned on the tele-visio-portal device. "Martin-Luther-Krankenhaus," he barked and immediately shut his eyes tight. Beads of perspiration erupted from the base of his temples. *Mein Gott,* how he hated this type of travel. Sometimes his memory got hazy and mixed up for days on end and his limbs felt as though they were molten rubber being cast into a mold not quite his size. The queasy feeling in his stomach just as he entered the space-time warp always made him think twice before he used the teleporter.

Eli rematerialized in the hospital's teleportal landing area. Approval for entry to the hospital zone came through quick enough, and he staggered into the sterile building. The travel extracted a lot of his strength and worry about his father ate away the rest. Images floated about, memory fusing into an abstract reality. He swayed for a moment and took a deep breath. He needed the few moments before his perception registered reality.

An array of transparent touchscreens stood silently awaiting inquiries about patients and the care center. Always preferring to talk to a human face, Eli walked past the automation to the receptionist and asked for his father's room. Drumming his fingers on the shiny counter, he waited while the perky, round-faced, smiling man at the desk tapped his screen for information. Apprehension etched a deep pain in his temples. *What happened to Papa? How did this happen all of a sudden?*

He glanced around. The professional look of the nurses gliding along on the clearly marked, smoothly moving walkways calmed him a bit. The receptionist thrust out a card with his father's room number and directions printed on it. Eli grabbed it and was about to turn and step on to the walkway when he noticed a small woman shuffle in, her disheveled brown hair flying in the draft created by the open hospital door. "Mutti! When did you get here? How's Papa?" he exclaimed. The halo of smoky odor that accompanied Antje announced the time she had spent with her cigarettes. Eli sighed and clenched his jaws tight. *Of course, she is nervous, but does she have to attack her lungs again?*

His mother raised her puffy eyes and took a couple of seconds to focus on him. Relief settled on her face, but her lips quivered. Tears and sobs were on their way. Antje turned back towards the door, beckoning him. No word left her mouth until they stepped out in the hospital garden.

"It is time." Antje's voice spewed out in a hoarse whisper.

Eli blinked. *Time for what?*

"It is time I told you about the curse," she said.

"Curse?" This was a strange diagnosis on her part. He stepped up and held his mother's forearms tight, trying to steady her. He needed to see his father and to see what could be done to help him, rather than this mumbo jumbo talk. Stress had clearly invaded his mother's sanity.

"The Bergmann family is cursed." Her voice trembled. It has been so for several generations. All the firstborn sons are struck with an incurable affliction and die. Your Papa will die the moment you turn twenty-one. That's the way it is." The last words almost didn't make it out of her throat.

Eli's heart beat faster as he heard the quiver and the pain in his mother's voice. *What in the world was she talking about?* Worse still, she really seemed to believe it. He shook his head, he could figure that out later, for now he needed to keep his perspective straight if he wanted to understand the situation and help his father if possible.

"But what is wrong with him, Mutti? Why aren't you telling me what happened?"

"Because I don't know, Elichen." Antje shrieked. "He just collapsed. The doctors cannot figure out what's wrong. They will not be able to. It is time. He is going to die. Die, do you hear?" Shaking, she held onto his forearms with clawed fingers. Her nails dug into his skin, penetrating through his sweatshirt. "It's the curse. It's the curse." She repeated, and then broke down into body shaking sobs accompanied by uncontrollable tears. For a moment, her eyes held on to the tears and then, as if a dam broke, they flowed down her cheeks and over her lips which were a quivering shade of paleness.

Over the next half hour, Eli with almost superhuman effort, pushed away a lurking suspicion about his mother's mental makeup, calmed her down. Then straightening his back, he walked stiffly over to his father's room and gently opened the glass door. The equipment, the large windows, and the sterile room made Emo's large body look frail. Blinking graphs on machines hooked to his father's body told the painful story about the slow decline of vital signs.

The doctor attending to Emo looked up as Eli approached. She wore a puzzled expression, eyebrows meeting in the center of her forehead. "*Nein!* I can't understand it!" she shook her head and murmured to no one in particular.

Later in a talk with Eli, she confided that she had given up hope of bringing Herr Bergmann back to the world of the living. To Eli, the world seemed to swing on hinges of ignorance. The doctor had practically washed her hands of Emo after a mere few hours. So had Antje who had taken to blubbering about some curses.

Eli stole a look at his father looking small in the large white bed. Dark circles had appeared under his father's eyes. His deterioration sped up as time passed. An invisible hand of worry snapped up from within and held Eli's throat. He gulped and looked up to see his mother near the tall windows still sobbing, though softly now. There seemed to be no dam to his mother's tears.

He then remembered his grandmother. "Mutti, did you inform Omi?"

She shook her head. "I asked the nurse to. But will <u>you</u> give her the details?" The words gushed out between loud sniffles. Eli nodded and glanced once more at the flashing screens around his father's bed. His jaw tightened. *What is wrong with these doctors? Can't they figure this out?*

"I'll be back soon, Mutti, I need some air." Eli, frustrated at the lack of diagnosis and his head whirling with the idea of curses, sprinted out of the hospital towards the Träger des Öffentlichen Transportmittels, TOT stop. The public transport vehicle wasn't due for another few minutes. His father's mysterious affliction, the doctors' apparent ignorance, his mother's sudden withdrawal into the remote world of witchcraft, all made him want to run away. Images of his father on his deathbed flashed through his mind like scenes from a badly made science fiction movie. Huge lumps of nothingness stuck in

Eli's throat. There didn't seem to be enough air to breathe.

Did it all make sense now, at the end of his father's road? All his childhood years when his father wanted to do everything with him, tell him all the stories he ever knew, darted through his mind. Looking back, normal doting now felt like the desperate effort by a man trying to make the most of his remaining time with his child. As though he was in a terrible hurry.

Tears threatened to well up in Eli's eyes. The entire situation with a healthy topping of guilt twirled up a volcano within him. He turned to a nearby trash can and threw up.

Later in the TOT, he gazed through the window, down at the ground flying past. The TOT glided a few meters above the ground, and this feeling of floating always gave Eli a different perspective on life. Today however, was different. Getting a better grasp of the situation was all he could think of. First, he needed to see his grandmother, who must be fraught with worry. She did not venture out of her house very much nowadays, content to tend to her garden. The trip to her home in the nearby town of Potsdam would have taken Eli about an hour by road and longer by the almost defunct trains. He tapped her address on his tele-visio-portal.

His Omi was in her garden when the connection came through. As the image appeared, Eli could feel the coolness of the garden on his skin. Bees buzzed around bright colored geraniums, honey suckles and cornflowers. Hunching over her prize-winning roses, her frail body and the silver cloud of hair around her head made her look more tired than usual. Her trembling hands betrayed her nervous frame of mind. Her face lit up when she saw his projection among her flowers. News of her son updated, Eli swallowed. "Er…Omi, there is something I need to ask you about the …er …curse." She looked up sharply. A sigh left her lips as he narrated his conversation with his mother. His grandmother's face showed resignation.

"Your mother told you the truth, *mein Bärchen*."

Eli smiled at her term of endearment despite her seriousness.

"Our family is cursed." His grandmother set down the pruning shears and looked straight into his eyes. "That is why I wanted your father to marry late. I wanted to keep him alive longer."

"What curse are you talking about, Omi?" Eli's voice reached a high decibel level. "This is not ancient mythology one reads in books. Curses don't happen in real life."

His grandmother's silver hair trembled in the light breeze. "Your grandfather died the day your father turned twenty-one, just like his father before him." She sighed. "Be with your father, *mein Bärchen,* for the last days. Spend time with him. That is all you can do for him. Do not waste time." She blinked back tears and managed to wring out a smile. "I will ask the good Herr Fiedler to drive me to the hospital, I will be there soon." She raised a wrinkled hand to her lips and blew a kiss at him. "*Tschüß!*"

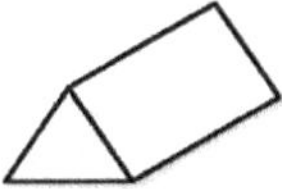

Now, a week later, the memory of the acidic bile taste was still fresh in Eli's mind.

Twenty-one hours remained.

The cross of nails caught a glint of flames from candles in the Gedächtniskirche ruins. Burning candles. A tradition that had lasted centuries. The flickering flames and the quiet of the church brought Eli the calm he needed after the week in the hospital. As days had gone by, the failure of doctors in providing a diagnosis had pushed Eli more towards faith. Agnostic by nature, he refused to accept the idea of curses, but he had nothing else to go on. He needed to talk to Omi once more, needed to find out more about the curse. This time however, he didn't want to just visually call on her. This time he needed to visit her in person, right away. He needed to be with her too and get a good old-fashioned hug. Before he turned twenty-one.

Only twenty-one hours remained.

He squinted in the semi-dark at his watch. Omi would leave for her evening prayers in thirty minutes. He pulled his tele-visio-portal device from his pocket. Two green bars blinked *Enough credit for two trips.* There and back. Zipping up his sweater, he glanced around. Tourists had started crowding into the church. Not wanting to be disrespectful, Eli whispered Omi's address into the portal device, took a deep breath, and clicked the start button.

For the second time in a week, the familiar, and immensely disgusting sensation of entering a space-time warp ran through his body. The only relief was that this time he was not rushing to a hospital but to his grandmother's cottage. A catch developed in his stomach and bile rose to his throat as his body trembled. He lost all sense of identity, of being, and of his body. It felt as though an eternity passed before he rematerialized.

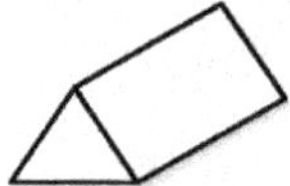

Eli blinked at soft sunlight streaming through the canopy of trees. *Is this Omi's garden?* The woods were dense, and his urban upbringing caused him to freeze at the unfamiliar sound of a brook and bird songs that sounded unusually loud and sharp. *Birds in Berlin?* He couldn't recall ever hearing them in the city. Maybe it was the rematerializing, he surmised. His clothes were in order, hands and feet, right. Yet, something was terribly wrong. *The portal miscalculated the address.* A clunk of wood on rock rang through the forest behind him. Staccato, it sounded more like footsteps. He breathed deep. *Okay, someone to check the location with.* He turned and the sight he saw almost knocked him down.

A gaunt woman, lantern in one hand and a cloth sling bag in the other, turned from behind a tree and faced him, face suddenly going pale. Dressed in a white hooded shirt and brown leather overalls, she would have reached Eli's waist at most. Her leather boots bore wooden soles. Her large brown eyes widened with fear and she staggered as Eli took a step towards her.

"*Wer!* Who are you? What are you?" she asked, her deep, almost masculine voice a raucous whisper and then she burst into a string of unfamiliar words. Her German dialect was old and forgotten, and Eli was happy for the language courses he took. He didn't know of anybody who still used such a language. He smiled at her. "I have a problem with my portal. I think it's broken."

The little woman blinked. Her expression conveyed a huge question mark. Clearly no information had gone through to her. He changed his questioning. "Where am I? Potsdam?" he asked. A small sign of recognition flected through the little woman's eyes. "*Ja, ja*, Potsdam!"

It was Eli's turn to be perplexed. He fished out his device. 1680, flashed in bright green. His brain raced through different possibilities. The problem was not space. The problem was time.

1680 A.D.! Instead of Gutenbergstrasse, he had arrived in the year1680. Another realization flashed in his mind. He was facing a *Wichtelweib*, one of the Zwerge races of Germany. All the hours at the library and the ancient books he had waded through finally paid off. A Zwerge was mythical. This person looked real enough. A mischievous race, the Zwerge used to torment miners, hurling stones at them, teasing them. He tilted his head and studied the dwarf's hands. No obvious weapons, no stones. A Wichtelweib's presence often meant rich ore beds around. Maybe there was a mine nearby. He glanced around and sighed. He was clearly in a forest. Moreover, whatever does a mine look like?

"I am a lost traveler," he said slowly, smiling, using his knowledge of the ancient dialect. Fatigue seeped into every pore of his skin. Teleporting sapped every ounce of his energy. Added to that was the extremely difficult challenge of communication. His eyelids drooped. She responded to his smile.

"I could try to get you back onto your path," she said. "You look tired and hungry, child." Her face softened with sympathy. "Would you like to go to my home and have a piece of bread?"

Eli gratefully accepted. He needed to get back to his Omi quickly, but some food wouldn't hurt. He didn't like to teleport on an empty stomach if he could manage it. The bread might help his extreme exhaustion.

About half an hour of silence followed with Eli treading along behind the Wichtelweib. Twilight set in, and black hues bled into the blue of the sky. Just when Eli thought he couldn't take another step, he spotted a dwelling. The little hut, part stone and part wood with a small half open door, stood behind the trees. Light flickered from within. She called out to someone and bounded inside. Eli, sensing that he should not enter the house uninvited, sat on a boulder outside. A bearded old Zwerge emerged, pipe in hand. Frayed suspenders held up his pants over a round belly. He blew out rings of smoke and sized Eli up. "Your name?" he asked in a deep voice similar to that of the female Wichtelweib.

"Eli Bergmann."

"Bergmann!" His voice boomed, startling Eli. His eyes narrowed and disappeared into slits in his cherubic face. "The cursed family." He spat into the clearing, turned and walked back into the house in a huff

Eli nearly fell off the boulder. His father was struggling for life, and here he was, centuries away, in a hallucinatory world, with a dwarf telling him that his family was cursed.

This must surely be a nightmare!

Eli's eyes filled with tears and he blinked. He heard that his family was cursed from his mother, then his grandmother and now these strangers. He breathed slowly trying to calm his confused mind. He waited a moment, walked up to the window and stuck his face to the glass pane. The elderly dwarf sat, red in the face, angrily puffing away at his pipe. The female Wichtelweib came to the door.

"Er...madam?" He wanted to know more.

"I'm Matilda," she answered, her face crinkling, as her mouth curved into a smile. She held out a plate with a quarter loaf of dark bread and a little jug of water.

"*Danke*!" Eli snatched the plate from her hand. He tore up the small crusty bread and thrust a piece into his mouth. Satisfaction spread through his body even though the bread tasted slightly stale. A quick gulp of water washed it down.

"*Frau* Matilda," he continued in a reverent manner and went on to explain as simply as he could, about how he got there and about his father. He had no sooner finished than Matilda sat down, facing him on the porch. She sat motionless for what seemed an eternity, apparently trying to digest the deluge of information that Eli had spewed. A sigh escaped her lips and she moved.

"The explanation is very simple. One of your ancestors was responsible for the death of one of my family. A little one."

Eli stared at her, shocked. "My ancestor murdered a child?"

The frown on Matilda's face and the scorn in her voice betrayed her feelings at a gross injustice committed several generations ago. "The mother of the child cursed him; he would die, and so will his firstborn son. To make sure that his family was destroyed the way her life had been."

Eli's mouth ran dry as the story sank in. Causing the death of children was quite a crime. Several things fell into place for Eli. He remembered that his ancestors were miners. Maybe, just maybe, in some strange way all of this made sense.

What horrible luck! Of all the Bergmann families in the world, he had to be born in the only one that was cursed.

"Hearing about the curse, Bergmann's wife came to us, flung herself onto the ground and begged for forgiveness," continued Matilda. "We may be different from you humans, but we have hearts too." Matilda's hoarse voice softened a bit. "My ancestor took mercy on the Bergmanns and said, 'I cannot take back my curse, but I can do this for you: Your husband will live until his firstborn turns twenty-one, and this will hold for the rest of the generations of your family.'" At this, Matilda paused. She swatted an insect absently before continuing, "And that is the reason why your father is dying. There is no way to save him, unless...."

Eli's eyes brightened. *There was an 'unless'!* In the world of man-made machines, his father was doomed. In this land of prehistoric magic, he had hope. "You mean there is a way to break the curse?"

"Of course, there is. There is always a way out." Matilda's eyes twinkled. "You humans are so easily dejected and scared that you stop thinking." Her merry cackle rang through the silent evening atmosphere.

"So...?" Eli asked, starting to be hopeful.

"It is not easy to do," Matilda said. "Before he turns twenty-one, the first born has to hand over to us that which is most precious to him."

Eli gulped. This was a revelation. But he had his questions. "Why did my ancestors not know of this?"

Matilda laughed. "Some did, but it is not easy to decide what is most precious." Then she added, "Another thing is that the son cannot die for the father."

Not knowing what else to do, Eli continued to munch the bread. He stood and scratched his head. His mind had numbed into an unthinking state. "*Danke schön*," he thanked her mechanically and turned away from the tiny dwelling.

As he walked into the woods, a deep throated chuckle

emanated from Matilda. *The sadist! She must think my situation is funny.* He kept walking, thinking and waiting for an idea to strike him. He needed to get back home, but he couldn't leave without at least trying now that he knew that a solution existed. This was good timing. He would turn twenty-one in a few short hours. Or maybe it wasn't, he would turn twenty-one in a few centuries. Even if he knew how to warp time in such a way that his previous generations weren't affected, he had no idea what was most precious to him. In any case, he did not have his belongings with him. What would he have given to this Wichtelweib if he did? He could not think anymore. All his books, his devices, his possessions seemed to be mere material crutches.

He walked for what felt like hours. Shadows darkened until they merged with the woods. Unfamiliar noises of the night reached his ears. A night in the forest was far different from a city night. An irrational spike of fear ran up Eli's spine. He turned and retraced his steps, squinting and concentrating to keep on the path. The darkness in the woods mirrored the darkness in his mind. No solution emerged.

He needed to ask Matilda if she had any clue as to what might qualify as the most precious thing. Maybe he could go back to his own time and try to return to the past with something precious. But would his device work again like it did this time? This present journey felt serendipitous and unrepeatable. He hoped the answer would come to him as he neared the

Wichtelweib's house.

By the time he reached Matilda's home, night settled in and the surrounding woods made it feel colder and darker. Matilda sat on the porch, in a rocking chair, a pipe in hand. She struck a match, lit her pipe and puffed deeply. Her face broke into a short smile as she noticed Eli draw near. Uneven teeth gleamed in the light of a lantern that swung from the roof.

"Have you finished thinking?" she hollered.

Eli winced.

The same loud, raspy voice. "I did not think you would return."

Eli came nearer. He felt defeated. "I really want to do something. If I give you what is precious to me, would this heal my father?"

Matilda cocked her head. A grunt emanated from within the hut. Evidently, her husband didn't like what he had overheard. She ignored him, as she would an insect on the wall. "I believe so. It is different because you belong so far away."

In time. Not space. "And what would happen to my forefathers if you restore my father right now? What about me?"

She shrugged. "Nothing, I suppose. I don't know." Then she added with a twinkle in her eye, "I think you will be all right."

Well, that's that. Now for the important part. "But I am so far from home, I don't have my belongings. I don't have anything to give you. " He dug his hands deep into his pockets to turn them inside out. His fingers felt the teleporter. "Except this, I guess," he added, looking down at the blinking, malfunctioning device.

It came to him in a flash. Maybe he could give her the teleporter. After all the *only* possession may also qualify as the *most precious* one.

But he needed it to get back and be with his father before the end, in the high chance that this magic did not work.

He needed it to get back. Period. He didn't want to be stuck in 1680.

But then, it was all he had.

Back and forth his mind swung. A few moments later he settled on a decision.

"This is all I have," he said, handing the teleporter to Matilda.

She squinted at the gleaming gadget, stood and removed the lantern from its hook. She brought it close to Eli's hand. "What is it? A box? What treasure does it hold?"

"Oh, it's no treasure box," Eli said, "It's what I used to come here. I don't know what you can do with it. It doesn't work, anyway."

Matilda strained her neck to scrutinize the teleporter without touching it.

"Go ahead, hold it," Eli encouraged. "Please take it. It's all I have."

She hesitated, then held out her hand and wrapped her fingers around it. She examined it curiously. "Without this, are you not bound to our time, *mein Kind*? This place. You will never see your father or your family again or live your life as you knew it."

"Yes, but my father will live." Eli said. "If you so wish."'

Matilda's face softened. She returned to her chair, placed the teleporter on her lap and rubbed it as she chewed her pipe. Several long moments passed before her voice boomed again.

"This indeed is the most precious thing you possess. Yes, your father will live. I wish so."

The sound of a glass breaking followed by a string of angry words emanated from within the hut. Matilda continued to rock herself, unconcerned. Eli let out a breath in relief. Her words made his head spin. He sat on cool earth in front of the porch. He did not know what to do, knowing he would always be stuck here. *Oh well. It could not be as bad as losing Papa.*

The ordeal was now over. Eli started shaking and to his shock he could not stop. To his even greater shock and shame, his bottled emotions came gushing through in the form of hot tears. He crouched closer to the ground to hide his miserable face from Matilda.

She approached him. Her hard, rough hand landed on his shoulder. He looked up, still shaking. Their eyes locked. A strange peace settled in him. He stopped shaking. He wiped his eyes with the back of his hand and a final sob escaped his lips. "I am sorry, it's just...it's just...."

Matilda shook her head.

She understands. He could never thank her enough or express how he felt.

Her wizened face broke into a sympathetic smile. "Your heart is pure, son. I will give you something which may help you with your life." She thrust her hand into her overalls pocket. Eli looked up, confused. She raised her arm and Eli saw her fingers move. Fine, sandy, golden dust poured out of her hand. Eli's eyes grew large when he saw Matilda's wrinkled face glimmering in the reflection of the gold. Maybe this would help him start anew. But before he could hold out his hands to receive the gift, Matilda whistled loud.

In a moment, a dust storm engulfed Eli. He closed his eyes tight. Sand whirled around him, entering his eyes, ears and mouth, and stinging his skin. *A tornado! I'm caught in a tornado.* His body stretched and twisted. The coarse sand scraped harder by the minute until Eli screamed in pain as pieces of skin were ripped off his body. The gritty powder filled his mouth and his efforts to spit it out in the midst of his screams were in vain. The torment raged for what seemed like hours. *Stop it, Frau Matilda! What are you doing to me?*

When he opened his eyes, Eli had materialized at the Gedächtniskirche. Candle flames danced in the sudden draft. *It was just a nightmare. Phew! How did I fall asleep here?* His throat was parched, and his neck felt sprained. His head throbbed, his eyes hurt, and his mind was in a fog. His entire body ached, and bruises had formed where sand had torn off his skin.

A faint hope rose slowly from the depths of his mind. Eli needed to get back to the hospital quickly. He patted his pockets for the teleporter.

A film peeled away from his mind as memories flowed in, like a deluge on parched earth.

Papa?

He could reach home quicker and contact the hospital from there. Eli ran.

"Ber…Ber…Bergmann!" Breathless after the fast sprint to his apartment, he spat into the voice recognition door lock. He rushed in, barely reached his living room as he reached out for the communicator and turned it on.

The face of the perky, smiling receptionist flickered into focus.

"Emo Bergmann, *bitte*. He has been in the center for a week," Eli breathed.

"*Ja. Ein moment, bitte.*" The receptionist's smile remained pasted on as he located the information. "Emo Bergmann. He will be released today."

Eli's face brightened. *Mathilda you didn't fail me*! "May I talk to him? I'm his son."

"*Ein moment,*" he murmured as he flicked the mute switch on and connected with Emo. Eli waited patiently as he watched the plump face grow redder, the smile turn from plastic to awkward and then fade away. The receptionist looked directly at Eli and with eyes flickering ever so slightly, cleared his throat and said, "He...sir, he doesn't have any memory of a son."

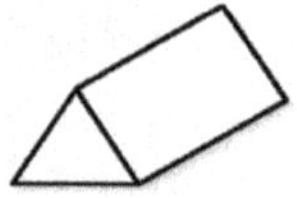

Once upon a time, Time spun around. Things were here yet they were not. It was then, yet it was not. And then it was ever after

Todd A. Walls

Todd A. Walls is a writer because of a truce. The stories that keep clamoring for attention will calmly await their turn, as long as Todd keeps writing them down. With the calm and quiet of Colorado's eastern plains outside—and the majestic Rocky Mountains marking the horizon—Todd's characters speak to him of their dreams and accomplishments, along with their failures and shame. Todd's imagination is a conduit to the end of time, riding the many failures of humanity to their impending outcomes, and embracing the heroic efforts of those who refuse such a fate.

Todd is the President of the Colorado Springs Fiction Writers Group (CSFWG.org). He lives in rural Colorado with his wife of 33 years, along with oodles of poodles, birds and cats. He currently works as an Information Security Consultant in the finance industry.

Contact Todd A. Walls:

www.toddawalls.com,

todd@toddawalls.com

https://www.facebook.com/Todd.A.Walls

The Digital Corpse

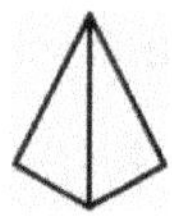

Lit-RPG Murder Mystery

by

Todd A. Walls

I palmed the door to my office on moonbase Colorado Springs, pausing a moment to appreciate the freshly painted sign, *Moser Consulting*. My girlfriend Kelly had to pout before I agreed to the title of consultant. "Never limit yourself by a name," she kept saying, "consultants can do anything." Once my handprint verified, it slid open.

After having solved the first murder on the moon, I became the most famous detective in the solar system. I admit, though, that Sherlock Holmes had me beat by a long shot. The current most-famous-detectives list had me at twenty-seven, two notches below Wishbone. Not that I had anything against Jack Russel Terriers, but I figured fictional detectives didn't count—not even the dogs that played them on TV. Among living detectives, I was on top.

My bio wasn't exactly celebrity material. Single female.

Professional investigator. Lives on the moon. Tall, dark, and pretty—forgettable, that is. Doesn't play well with others.

"Hey, Jazzy," Kelly said, draped across a comfy chair next to my desk like an inviting blanket on a cool night. "How's my girl?" After setting down the tablet she was reading, Kelly stretched from head to toe, fingers running through her blond hair in a whole-body wave of sensuality that left me breathless. She probably hadn't even done it on purpose.

That's just her style.

Like always, I couldn't help but admire how comfortable she seemed in her own body. Kelly and I were nothing alike. She had the confidence, the angelic face with one tiny freckle just above her right eye that reminded me she was human, and the only one of us with a steady paycheck. She was a Fed, and for another few months, my probation officer.

Our office was also our home. On the moon, things rarely had a single purpose, not even people. In the last year, I had worked in construction, entertainment, education, and most recently as an investigator. Mostly with success. Well, not including my ill-fated attempt to win a poker tournament. My biggest contribution to entertainment—and true claim to fame— was when I led law enforcement on a high-speed chase across the lunar surface in a crotch rocket moon bike with no brakes. Ask me sometime about my stand-up act. It's a killer.

So now you know why I have a probation officer. Kelly's also the agent who was in the chase car, bless her heart. Don't let her fool you, she loved every minute of it except for the part where she knew she might have to shoot me. We don't talk about that.

"Check your messages," Kelly said. "You got something from Governor Tarkin."

"Just because Governor *Sheldon* wouldn't grant me a pardon doesn't mean he's running an evil empire," I said, reaching for my deskpad computer. "Hey. You read my mail, didn't you?"

"Somebody's gotta keep a close eye and make sure you don't stray to the dark side. It would really burn my butt to have to arrest you. Again."

"I promise you'll be arresting me before we go to sleep, tonight." I grinned, bringing up the governor's message. "You might even have to search me for contraband."

"I can always hope." She got up, walked across the room, and leaned against the bedroom doorframe, perversely giving me privacy to read a message she had already read.

Sheldon was the governor of Colorado's territory on the moon, and we were actually on pretty good terms. Every state and nation on Earth had an allotted slice of the moon, like an off-world annex. My office was in the Colorado Springs complex. The message was text only but came with an encryption certificate that identified it as an official government communication. "Hmm. That's why he didn't just send me a text. Must be important." I looked intently at Kelly. Now I knew why she had stepped away. She was acting guilty. "How did you read a digitally encrypted email? Do you have my password?"

"A girl never reveals her secrets," she bit her lip and blinked her eyes dreamily. This was no accident. "But since you caught me already, someone's dear diary sure knows a few juicy secrets," she grinned.

"Kelly, that's magicians. Magicians never reveal their secrets. Lovers do. In case you forgot." I shook my head, I hated it when she got intrusive. But then, she had read my diary and it did, indeed, contain some secrets. Jaz felt a twinge of guilt. "We'll talk about this later."

Kelly caressed the doorframe just long enough to steal my breath, and then slid into the bedroom, fingers last, wiggling at me.

Now my curiosity was brimming. The message said, *"Case for you, Jaz. Meet Mr. Sterling at the AHCCC next opportunity. He'll take you to the corpse. PO:122-3764228. Keep a lid on it. Sheldon."*

I raised my voice so Kelly could hear. "Dang, he's got a purchase order on file already. There's a corpse!" Assuming the death was unlawful, this would be the second off-world murder in human history. It seemed a bit disrespectful to be so excited over a person's untimely death, but this is what I lived for.

I raised my voice so Kelly could hear me in the next room. "I sense some on-the-job expenses coming up in about ten minutes." I tapped out a request for a vehicle on my deskpad. It would take us hours to walk to the Asimov High-Capacity Computing Center through a combination of underground tunnels and surface trails. The computer center was in the Denver Complex, and corpses had an expiration date, so to speak. Better drive there right away.

I looked up and pointed to the bedroom, where I kept my usual sleuthing tools. "Hey, Kelly, could you get my--" She was already standing next to me, hooking the bag over my arm.

"I freshened up your test kit. Batteries are good. I packed your extra data drive in case you need to get a forensic image of a system," Kelly said, handing me a set of thermal underwear. "And your fur-lined panties, 'cause you know you always get cold in a moon suit."

"You're despicable, or lovable, I'm not sure which. You knew about this all along." I accused. "You should have texted me at the very least. I could've gotten back sooner."

"I wasn't sure you'd be interested," she play-pouted.

I smirked. "Bloody unlikely."

"Okay." Kelly smirked back. "You needed to submit your business license in order to file for expenses for the office. If I texted you, then you might have come back without filing it, and then you wouldn't have been reimbursed for the car you just reserved."

"God." I shook my head. "You are so damn right. I hate you." I set the bag down on the desk chair and slid into her arms. A sigh became a kiss, and a kiss became an epic battle between haste and desire.

I stopped, and then kissed her several times in quick succession.

"We really need to go," she breathed.

I couldn't even speak, just nodded and picked up my bag.

First stop was a locker next to the main building airlock. Lockers were for public use and shared. The suits were not. Everyone on the moon had at least one pressure suit that had been custom fitted and sometimes custom made.

I looked Kelly over as she fastened a boot. She always denied it, but nobody looked that good in a moon suit unless it'd been custom made. My suit had adjustable straps and each part was pieced together to fit in the standard way. The arms, legs, torso, boots, and even the gloves were all my size. Especially the gloves, which were the only part you would call custom made. I could shuffle cards in these gloves, but they had cost me a fortune.

Kelly's suit fit her like my gloves from head to foot. I was a tiny bit jealous. So which was better? To look like that, or to sleep with that? Hard to say. As it was, I decided I had the best part of the bargain. I wouldn't like the kind of attention that Kelly got everywhere she went. It's nice to be able to sit in a corner and go unnoticed, especially on a case.

I took a deep breath, which I knew was a completely irrational habit, and snapped my helmet into place.

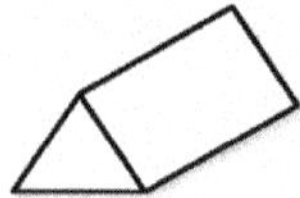

Driving an electric two-seater rolly, the two of us retraced the route of our epic car chase from the year before, from el Colorado Springs to el Denver. The el being slang for "L" or lunar. The stolen moon bike I had used the first time had better acceleration, but this spherical rolly was both more comfortable and a lot safer to drive. It could turn on the point of a pin. Or—more accurately—it could rotate the inner passenger assembly along with the drive train and resume acceleration in any given direction.

Staying suited was cheaper than paying for atmosphere inside the bubble. The government would consider that a luxury, and I wanted to save any arguments over professional expenses for something more important, like an upgraded room, or a king-sized bed. Unfortunately, the suits also put a barrier between us.

Kelly patted my leg and then pointed to the terrain indicator on the dash. Her voice came over the encrypted RF link in our helmets. "Hey girl, you got a paparazzo."

"I thought they were called paparazzi."

"Yeah, but you only got the one."

I twisted around and saw a space drone catching up with us from behind. Atmospheric drones don't work on the moon. It resembled an old west wagon wheel with a big pot of stew on top. The craft sported six small reaction engines attached to spokes along its axis. The black pot was a fuel tank. Slung underneath was a black camera pivoting on the end of a thin armature.

"Hmm, reaction mass is expensive, but it can go anywhere it wants to." I mused. "You think this is from a sleazy tabloid or a mainstream network? I don't know whether we would get more headlines from pretending to argue or from doing a little suit nookie. Wanna play?"

Despite my easy banter, my innards were roiling with every possible feeling. My first time along this road was a desperate flight for life that ended in almost killing myself with a severe concussion. The second trip, to my sentencing hearing, was the most humiliating and longest perp ride in history. They had insisted on keeping me handcuffed the whole ride. Both trips had been covered by every media source with a lunar affiliate. On the positive side, I had good ratings on both occasions. My YouTube comedy channel still generated a nice income stream. Famous, infamous, same difference.

Kelly eyed the device for a moment, which passed us and peered in through the front. "Save your acting skills for another time. That's an unmarked government model, but I don't think it's FBI. I don't know who that would be. It has upgrades attached to the hub, but I don't recognize them."

A few minutes later, we caught up to a unicycle-style land cam. It waited until we got close and then matched our speed, bouncing along the right side of the road. The camera it held was bulkier but stayed steady on top of a piston that compensated for the rough ground. By then, the other drone had disappeared.

"I recognize the markings on this one," I said. "Network conglomerate. I wonder who snitched on the case? Or do you think they monitor this road all the time, now?"

Kelly nodded. "They do more than just monitor. Besides, it's hard to keep a dead body secret. I've been listening on a side channel. There's a Twitter feed trending called hashtag MoonDenverCrimeScene, though no one can agree on where— exactly—the crime scene is. Everything isn't about you."

"Are you sure? 'Cause it seems like it is."

Lackluster media coverage wasn't the only difference. I had noticed a few other changes along the way. At several choke points through rough terrain, there were heavy barricades that could block the path. As we passed another one, I noticed boulders had been repositioned to deter alternate routes.

"You know," I smirked, "this was a nice neighborhood until the riffraff moved in."

"No," Kelly answered. "I think it was about the time you arrived. Don't let it go to your head. Felon."

"Federali."

"Chika."

"Fresa."

"Hey," Kelly said. "I will stop this car right now and spank you in front of the evening news. Shut your mouth. I'm not like that. Much."

"I'd say I'm not that much of a felon, either, but I got off pretty light, considering." I said.

Kelly sighed. "Do you have any idea how awkward it is to be a high-profile federal agent dating the Moon's most notorious criminal?"

I chuckled. "I'm the Moon's only notorious criminal. The minute I stop being useful around here, they'll have me on the next shuttle planetside."

Kelly shook her head and didn't reply for a moment. When it came, her response was chilly. "And how, exactly, does that take me out of your spotlight?"

Another wheeled robocam caught up to us, this one bouncing along on the left side of the road.

"See? There's two of them, now. Paparazzi," I said. "And don't give me that. You know you *love* the attention."

Kelly twisted in her seat and glared at me a moment. As her attention returned to the road, I saw a glimmer of a grin. "Love is overrated."

After checking our suits into public lockers, we were met by an escort inside the Asimov High-Capacity Computing Center She was an elderly woman named Fender who broke all my expectations for a computer nerd. Her nametag said she was a Database Engineer, but she must have come from a very unusual family Fender's hair was scarlet red and cascaded in large curls to her lower back. On her neck was a tattoo of a large black hand with claw-like nails that appeared to be choking her and blood streaming down from rips in the flesh. One might assume that the hand wasn't quite so—wrinkled—when it was first imprinted.

"We just passed the main computer room. Where is the body?" I asked.

Fender stopped in the middle of the hallway and looked in every direction before answering. "Look, I'm sorry for all the secrecy. I don't know fully what's going on, but my boss has made it very clear that any leaks will mean my job, for starters. He mentioned jail, so, no hints until I hand you off to the GM. Stop asking."

"GM? You mean like a gamemaster? Why's that?"

"See. I've already said too much." Our guide led us around the corner to an elevator and pushed the down button. "You'll know soon enough."

After reaching the second basement level by elevator, we walked across the hall to a stairway that continued down. On the moon, multiple basements were par for the course. Still, the stairs didn't end for another three levels, the deepest lunar building I had ever been in.

Fender led us into a room. The simply appointed office, devoid of any character or signs of frequent use, only served to deepen my unease. Several cardboard boxes filled one corner. The only furniture was a desk that had seen better days. There were no tables, no clock, not even a chair. On the desk lay two clipboards holding non-disclosure forms, and two pens. One said Jazzy Moser. I took that one and handed the one for Kelly Scott to my partner.

"Kelly, what's this about a federal offense? Is this for real?" The document was a strongly and clearly worded plea for silence.

Kelly answered, "I've signed these before. In fact, as a federal agent I shouldn't have to sign one at all, unless it's for an external agency. It's a boilerplate form. I wouldn't worry too much about it. As long as you keep your mouth shut, you should be fine." She smirked and glanced at Fender, who also smirked. "Of course, if you act like your normal self then you might have a problem."

"Hey," I signed the paper with a flourish that covered half the page, and then slammed the clipboard back down on the desk. "I don't have any problems keeping a secret, but I don't participate in cover-ups. I'll keep the truth to myself if that's what I need to do, but I won't lie for the FBI if it comes to that."

"I'll keep that in mind."

Fender clapped, "Awesome! You're going to love this. Have you ever played *Mars Attacks?* It's a spin off from that old movie. Humans go to Mars and basically do to them what they did to Earth in the movie. It's a blast. With a blaster, even, depending on your character class."

Kelly said, "We play it. A little too much, sometimes."

Opening the door in the back of the office, Fender led us to another room. This one contained six immersion cocoons, three on each side, and a coffee pot on a table against the far wall, full of what smelled like freshly brewed coffee. My mouth watered.

"I love the way the game combines scientific exploration with public media," I said. "You gotta love it when digital fiction meets reality."

"Yes," Fender nodded. "And more importantly, the entire game world is generated from telemetry as it's sent in real time from the Mars Rover exploration program. A lot of the game takes place in the subterranean tunnels they found, but a lot of science does, too. That's why we have these immersion pods at the computer center. It's a cooperative program between us, the International Space Agency, the game developer, and the University of Lunar Colorado."

"Cocoons," I corrected.

"Cocoons," Fender nodded. "That's what the manufacturer calls them, but I spend a lot of time with students. They call them pods. In any case, we've got a team of graduate students analyzing the recently discovered Mars tunnel complex. I think we'll see at least half a dozen successful dissertations on ancient aliens here in the next year or two. The students are really pissed we commandeered these rooms. They spend more time on Mars than they do on Earth."

Kelly laughed. "That's wild. Who would have thought we'd see students getting PhDs in the field of ancient aliens? It's not just for nut cases, anymore."

"Hey," I complained, motioning at myself. "A little sensitivity, here? Just because I watch the History channel doesn't make me a nut case. Besides, a lot of that stuff has already turned out to be true."

"Pick a pod, any pod." Fender said. "I tried to wipe down everything. After so many hours of use, they get a little gamey, and some of the students' priorities don't include daily hygiene. A little hint, though, I spent most of my time cleaning units one, two, and three. I wasn't sure how many of you were coming until a couple of hours ago."

"Okay, time out," I said shaking my head, and setting my tool bag down next to the coffee pot, the scent of which was nearly winning the war for my attention. "This is all very interesting, and I love a good MMORPG as much as the next girl, but if you're cleared to tell us now, where the hell is the body?"

Fender shook her head. "You'll need to enter the game to find out. I just can't say any more right now because I don't know a whole lot more. In my opinion, I don't think anybody knows."

"As long as it isn't a dead Martian." Kelly interjected. "At this point I'm ready to believe anything."

Fender laughed, hard.

In fact, it was a tiny bit spooky how hard she laughed.

"No. No, it's not an alien body. Nobody's found any alien corpses lying around. Not yet, anyway. But I am working on a second master's in comparative physiology. If somebody does find an alien stiff, I want in on it. *So bad.*"

That last part came out in a whisper. I was starting to like our biker-nerd guide who was certainly named after a guitar. I almost wanted her to be my grandmother.

Like or not, my patience was wearing about as thin as the atmosphere on Mars. "Where. Is. The body?"

Fender sighed deeply. "I honestly don't know where the body is, but the corpse is in the game. For that, you'll need to talk to Technovamp Straad. Real name is Avi Sterling. He's the head game master. Suit up."

I eyed the coffee pot and decided that the corpse wouldn't be any more dead if I took a moment for a quick cup. Coffee was incredibly expensive to lift out of Earth's gravity well. Be a shame to let it go to waste. I lifted the pot and breathed the fresh aroma as deep as possible before pouring it into a cup.

I took the first sip, and as the crisp, bright acidity dissipated across my tongue, I closed my eyes and said, "I think I'm in love." Glancing at Kelly, I added, "Definitely not overrated."

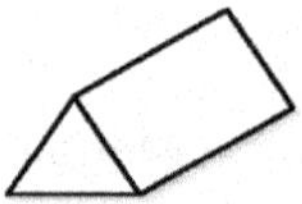

Though the game company had prepared new user accounts for us, upon realizing our characters would be level one, Kelly and I both opted to log into our own accounts. Upon entry, the game deposited us at the site of our last quest together, in front of the non-player character Taleous Deadeye, who had awarded us both with a minor Heal-Over-Time "HOT" clicky with unlimited charges. From here we had a good view of the Bloodfields zone at the foot of Mount Olympus.

The Bloodfields held a great army camp, which in turn held a great many Martians. It was a good quest zone, and a great raid zone. It would be fun to be in the opposing raid force once my level dinged into three digits. We weren't noobs, but we weren't up with the high-level raiders yet, either. We spent a lot of time here taking out scouts and messengers in the surrounding area. Kelly avoided the main army completely, but my stealth skills netted me loads of crystalline shards from pickpocketing the sleeping guards. Those went for a premium in the marketplace.

Don't get me wrong, it was dangerous, here. If you ever got aggro in the main camp, you had better have a few dozen friends to back it up or an evac spell. There was one other escape route, death. Still, I hated the experience loss from dying and neither one of us was a priest class for the rez, or resurrection, which restored lost experience points if you could get it. As careful as I was, Kelly was still three levels above me. I tended to die a lot, but I was rich in the game from all the trading.

Kelly's character was a human Bloodwing, a high-tech ninja class with spiderweave armor and dual-wielded crystalline blades. Her game name was Alphadog, a name that gave me endless opportunities for teasing. Her gear consisted of dark gray self-spun spidersilk that wrapped her voluptuous body as tightly as her spacesuit. Kelly does have a certain style.

After spending an embarrassing number of hours in front of a crystallization forge, Alpha now had a full set of player-crafted crystalline boomerang shurikens. Those babies could rip through tier-two armor like tissue paper. Only raid dropped armor of tier-three or higher had any hope of negating damage, making her a bit of a hustler in the dueling arena. Not many players accepted her challenge more than once, unless they were in a high-end raiding guild with a twinked alternate account, making them equivalent hustlers.

My character was a human Shadowrogue, an assassin class with a sniper skillset and a specialty in explosives. My game name was Sleepkiller, and you can take one guess whose sleep she was killing, though most people thought it referred to my character's preferred time for assassinations. I hadn't bothered to develop any crafting skills, since Kelly had already achieved her grandmaster crafting trophy. Anything I needed to make was her department, and I sprayed crafted grenades like a firehose when things got tough. Much of my game time was spent farming components for Alphadog's crafts.

I was what you would call a paper tank. Almost any player or mob near my level could pretty much single-shot me into the afterworld, but they had to catch me first. From a distance, I was deadly, and if you got too close, you'd find out firsthand how much time I had spent skilling up in explosives.

No raiding guild with any kind of standards would take us yet, since I was level eighty-six and Kelly eighty-nine. You had to be one hundred plus to even apply to most of them, but our goals were more about grouping together and completing cooperative quests. Neither of us were interested in the full-time commitment required of the top guilds. Besides, living on the moon isn't cheap. We had to spend most of our time making a living. That pot of coffee back in the real world would have cost me half a day's work. Fortunately, I wasn't the one paying the tab today.

"Hey," the place had changed drastically. "What the heck happened to Mount Olympus?"

"For that matter," I moved close to inspect a nearby rock dwelling, and then came back up to Alphadog. "What happened to everything?"

All around us trees, rocks, NPCs, and even the slopes of the great Martian volcano were paint tagged like some post-apocalyptic inner-city ruin. GMs probably had some way of erasing anything overly profane, but some of it was pretty rude—and graphic.

Alphadog responded, "What did they do? Institute a guns-for-spray cans trade program? This place looks like somewhere good girls shouldn't go."

"Since when have you been a good girl?"

A player running up to NPC Taleous, a nearby Non-Player-Character quest giver, must have overheard the comment, and told us. "Dude, it was the first anniversary in-game festival last week. They handed out paint cans as party favors and set up the game so you could paint anything. Well, anything except for other players."

The player turned back to Taleous and said, "Hail, Taleous Deadeye."

Taleous responded, "Welcome adventurer. I've been studying the properties of plants on the slopes of the nearby mountain."

"What plants?" The player asked.

I tuned out the game dialog that followed. I had done the same quest a dozen times already. "*Seriously?*" I typed in a player tell that would go only to Alphadog. "*What part of this idiot makes him think I'm a dude?*"

An emote showed up in my main chat window, in bright yellow text: *Alphadog thinks your character forgot to change her wardrobe after her last cyber session.*

Punching the function key to change the visual angle to self-view, I saw a tall ebony goddess wearing a diaphanous wrap over nothing but bright yellow panties and a matching bra. I didn't look like any sort of guy.

Another emote: *Alphadog is giggling.* And then, *Dude.*

Looking at my hotkey bars, I realized I had somehow rotated through to a little used set of keys. I had thought I was activating the forage skill, which was pure habit by now, and had accidentally hit the hotkey that changed out all my armor to an auxiliary set. Specifically, the set I used in private moments with my girlfriend. I clicked again, and all my gear changed out to my normal battle set, which effectively disguised most of the curves of my character with drab gray shapeless cloth armor. Our armor was dyed the same color, but Kelly and I looked nothing alike.

I typed an emote: *Sleepkiller is considering an assassination attempt on her girlfriend for not telling her she was NAKED.*

I found the right hotkey bar, double-checked it was the correct one, and then hit *forage* a lot harder than was necessary. After a few seconds, I saw a game message, "*Sleepkiller has successfully foraged a desiccated mushroom.*"

The other player ran off on his plant quest.

Alphadog said aloud, instead of typing privately, "As if you could take me."

Switching the camera angle back to normal, I opened my inventory and found the Stein of Endless Knowledge, a prize I had won at a slot machine in the game casino. Alpha didn't have one yet. I right-clicked it for a free teleport to the Isle of Knowledge, where we were supposed to meet Gamemaster Straad. It had unlimited charges but was slow as molasses in moon gravity. Molasses is slow on Earth. On the moon, it was excruciating. The port spell emitted a shrill tell-tale crescendo of sound audible to all nearby players.

"Are you teleporting?"

While I was trying to think of a suitable comeback, my screen went black and said: *Entering the Isle of Knowledge.* I had left her behind.

She could find her own damn way.

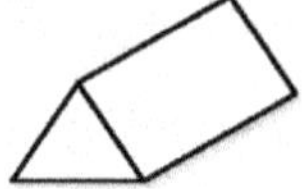

The *Mars Attacks* game was a mixture of science fiction and fantasy. In a homage to the author Arthur C. Clarke, game lore held that players could cast spells based on a sufficiently advanced technology that was indistinguishable from magic. In this lore, a high-end ray gun was not necessarily more powerful than traditional Japanese shuriken with atom-sharp edges and the high-tech ability to fly back to their owners.

The Isle of Knowledge was large enough that I couldn't see the ocean of dust surrounding it from the zone-in spot. On Mars, an island was more of a mound of bedrock poking through the ever-present regolith. It held numerous buildings and walled off boroughs surrounding a giant central library, hence the name Isle of Knowledge. There were no Martians here and every faction had its own borough, making this an ideal meeting spot.

Dozens of players stood around in the central square around a fountain of green water. Most of them had the letters AFK floating above their heads, indicating they were out of their cocoons and away from the keyboard. It wasn't just a good meeting spot, but also a good parking spot. Buffs were frozen here so they didn't count down, and players would often cast beneficial effects on all the characters present. You could stop for dinner and come back to find your character all buffed up and ready to rock.

Normally, players are difficult to track down beyond what zone they're in, but Kelly had set me up with a third-party macroing system with its own special built-in commands. I typed, "/target Straad," and a red dot on my in-game map showed me he was in a nearby building. Being a two-dimensional map, I couldn't tell which floor he was on. The building was at least three stories above ground, and most buildings in this game had a basement and a sewer level.

Next, I typed, "*/find target.*" A sparkly meandering path appeared. I followed it to what looked like an average NPC looking out of a second-floor window. "Game Master Straad, I presume?"

He turned to me and said, "Hullo, adventurer. What brings you to the Isle of Knowledge?" It was a southern accent, hitting the 'you' with such a high note that his voice cracked a little.

"Cut the act. I'm Jaz. Nice disguise. You look just like a merchant."

"I was told you'd been given a different character," Straad said.

It was an abrupt transition from the southern accent to one from across the pond from Earth-Colorado, or e-Colorado, where I had grown up. Game HQ was in e-London, though he could be physically anywhere, just as I could. I guessed that he was a native Englishman.

I said, "You didn't expect us to wear baby clothes did you. Level one? That's just plain rude. I bet you could make me max level in a second if you wanted." I moved my character, Sleep, up close and strafed sideways until our characters were eye to eye.

Straad answered, "If I wanted."

"It was worth a shot."

"How did you track me down so fast? Shadowrogues can sneak, but they can't track."

Turning to look out the window, I spotted Alphadog spinning in place at the portal. She must have burned a teleport scroll to get here so fast. Served her right. "Oh," I said, hoping to change the subject, "My partner's here." Before I could text her our location, Alpha headed straight for the door below us.

"She with you? She's a, let's see, a Bloodwing. Also not a tracker. You two wouldn't be violating the user agreement with third party software, right?"

"I'm on the clock. Do you want me to solve this case or quibble over a hotkey or two?"

"Sorry. Habit." Straad folded his arms. "But most players don't track me down so easy. Just saying."

Alphadog ran through the door into the room. "I had to drink my last Draught of Knowledge to port myself here. You could have grouped us for the port you know."

So, she had used a potion instead of a scroll. Those are instant-cast, and much more expensive.

"Oh, we weren't grouped? Here." I sent group invites to Straad and Alphadog and enabled group voice chat so that we could speak amongst ourselves without nearby players hearing. They both readily accepted.

"So, this the guy?" Alpha asked.

"Yes, GM Straad, meet Kelly, my partner in crime. Or rather, in solving them. So. Tell us about this alleged murder." I said, via voice chat.

"In a sec," said Straad. "Ah, Moser and Scott. Month-to-month, I see."

"Do you have any idea how much a subscription to this game costs?" Alphadog asked. "You're lucky we were loyal enough not to bail out for a free emu server."

"I was going to say," Straad flickered and all of his drab clothing was replaced by cherry red plate armor. "That I could give your accounts free access for the duration of the investigation, if that's all right?"

I nodded, "That's acceptable." Through a private text, I told Alphadog, *"He knows we use macro plugins, and he also knows our account names. Cool it. We don't want to get perma-banned for cheating."*

"So," Alphadog said, "What's next?"

"Next, I show you some of *my* hotkeys," Straad posed with a flourish. "Sorry, wrong time for that kind of humor, I guess. You know, those emulation servers run off a pirated copy of the game. No updates. We update every day at noon, London time, with the latest downloads from all three fleets of Mars rover databases. Every day we open up new territory. Players get to explore a brand new world as it's discovered. We're kind of proud of the setup."

"Your marketing spiel is great, but we're already convinced." This silent treatment was beginning to get old. "We play the game. What I don't understand is why we're *in* the game. I thought this was an investigation, not a game quest. You gotta give me something."

"We hear you're pretty good with computers."

"Thanks. I mean, I've done some programming. Kelly's the real deal. Between the two of us, we're not too shabby."

"Listen, I'd rather not talk here. Let's go somewhere with some privacy." His character gestured grandly. "Incoming."

I barely heard the tinkling of a portal spell before the words, *"Entering Customer Service Zone"* floated in front of me. This was no molasses-slow portal spell, especially since only employees would be using it. The scene dissolved to black and then to an ancient great hall lined with NPCs, flickering torches, and robots. Stars shone through large plate glass windows. It was anachronistic, like a spaceship dressed up for a costume party. Thanks to my custom mapping macro, I knew the characters and robots were NPCs by the black dots representing them on the map.

"Crud, I knew there had to be a zone like this somewhere in the game." Alphadog said. "Are we somewhere on top of Mount Olympus, game wise?" She ran over to look out a window.

"We're in a low-orbit space station over Mars," Straad said.

"Not modeled, of course. They aren't projected to have a real space station over Mars for a couple of decades. Its altitude is way above the visual cutting plane, though." He gestured to indicate the entire structure. "The station's invisible from the ground."

"Interesting." I glanced around, and then back to Straad. "We have privacy. Spill it."

"We have a player that appears to be either dead or helpless." Straad shrugged. "Problem is we don't know where the player's logged in from. Your job is to help us find him—or her. First stop is the tunnels where the player's avatar is comatose, then I'll take you to grill the devs for any technical details you may need."

Alphadog laughed, walking over to stand with us. "We grill suspects, not the experts." She paused. "Unless you think one of the devs is a suspect?"

The space vampire shrugged, "I have no idea. That's your department. My department is helping you out with gear, or whatever you think you need to conduct your investigation. I have constraints, too. Mainly from the government. I can't figure out why they're so concerned about this case."

"Which government?" Alpha asked, twisting a little to the side, not coincidentally placing her feet together, throwing one hip out. Looking back over her shoulder at him, she twirled a bit of hair, as if only half interested in his answer. The cocoon picked up on body movements and translated them into the game, and body movements were her specialty.

I suspected that particular game pose had resulted in more than one offer of a date—before my time, of course. Somehow, even though I had a great body in the game, I never got the hang of making it come alive. I'm pretty sure she spent hours practicing her moves while I was farming and pickpocketing shards to fuel her master trade skills. To each their own. She was sexy. I was rich.

Straad was, evidently, not impressed. "You might want to check out the gnome vendor over by the fireplace. She has potions of UltraVision, an Eye of Zona, and other items that you might need to explore the game world in ways that most players," he tilted his head and finished the thought, "or detectives can't."

I ran over to the girl gnome and checked her vendor inventory. "Hey, this stuff is all free!"

The Technovamp laughed, "True, but the good stuff is no-trade, no-drop, and temporary. It'll disappear as soon as you log out of the game. We use many of these items for GM events and special holiday quests. You can't get them without a GMs help. You're welcome."

"Crap, it's good to be the GM," I marveled. "You got any job openings?"

"No." The speed and tone of his answer told me he got that question often.

Looking through the vendor inventory, I found powerful

stat food and drinks that weren't temporary and loaded up with a dozen stacks of each. After eating and drinking them, it would boost my hit points and double my natural healing regen for four hours. That's helpful when you don't have a full cleric or medic in the group. This game area was like a candy store for developers and Game Masters, and I had been given a free ticket. I went from vendor to vendor buying up everything in sight. Much of it was temporary, but I didn't plan on logging any time soon if I could help it. The only thing stopping me was when my bags were full. I eyed the last few vendors longingly but decided I had taken long enough.

Time to get to work. "Alpha, you done yet?"

"No, I'm not done yet. If I was, I would have told you."

I felt a little bit of smugness that I was prepared to move on before she was. And then I was a tiny bit ashamed at the relentless competition between us. Nothing was too small or petty to try and win. I suppose it came from us being—at the beginning—on opposite sides of the law. Undoubtedly, Alpha was running around like crazy trying to find something better than I found to make up for coming in last.

While I waited, I put on the clothing that I had found. Temporary or not, the stats and effects of it were through the roof.

"I'm done," Alphadog pumped up on tiptoes, waving her arms for balance like a cross between ballerina practice and a Tyrannosaurus Rex trying to look innocent.

"Oh, my." I breathed. "Ohhhh, my."

My sexy Bloodwing girlfriend had ditched her black painted-on look for an enormous neon pink adamantium breastplate and greaves. On the chest were enormous, um, spikes. Two of them in case I wasn't clear. Leggings consisted of long, white furry chaps over bare skin, and her head sported a fluffy white peacock tail fanning out from one side to the other.

I busted a gut. I mean, my god, I was in tears.

"Ooh, wow," I said. "If you're seriously going out in public looking like that, we are totally even for you not telling me I was naked." I hooted a few more times. I hate my laugh because when I get going, I sound like a blacksmith's bellows. I was laughing so hard I could barely get out the words, "Because, that, is, so, much worse." I squeezed my eyes shut, shaking my head.

Straad, looking for the world like he was chewing on his tongue to keep from laughing, said, "Are we ready now?"

"Ooo, we're done. Aren't we, Sleepy," crooned Alpha.

Straad shook his head, and said thoughtfully, "I knew all those things existed, but I never saw them put together quite like that. Interesting look."

It's common to shorten game names to the first syllable or two. While most PCs call me Sleep, only Kelly calls me Sleepy, like I'm one of the seven dwarves for God's sake. "It's time to use our serious faces." I passed my palm across my face. "Time to work." Laughter bubbled up again and kept me from talking. The thought of her trying to use a serious face in that getup was ludicrous.

"Never mind," I said with a stopping motion. "Let's get to the crime scene before you break out your balls."

Straad looked at me, questioningly, then raised an eyebrow.

"You know, and start juggling," I couldn't kill the grin if I tried. "She juggles. A waste of perfectly good skill points."

"Incoming port," was his only answer.

The jingling sound of an incoming portal spell, was followed quickly by, "Entering The Shrieker Caves."

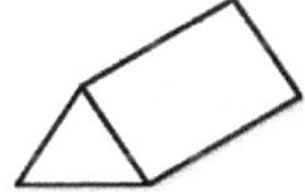

The zone-in location was underground. The Shrieker Caves was one of the newer zones being freshly explored by the rovers. Crowds of players usually adventured through here to experience the new content. I didn't care for it. The mobs here made my skin crawl. Ferocious bats dived for your hair before planting their fangs in your neck and shrieking in your ear. You were lucky if you didn't pick up some sort of disease.

The cocoons, or pods, whichever you prefer, had shoulder pads with dull spikes that tensed my whole back when they poked my neck. I didn't plan on letting anything get within bite range this time. I ate a Miraculous Picnic and an Ancient Fizzer from inventory, courtesy of Customer Service, and two four-hour timers appeared in my buff bar shaped like cornucopias. For the next four hours I would be stronger, harder to hit, and more agile. "Let's get to work," I looked around anxiously. Usually the mobs in this zone dropped instant aggro at the zone line. Game designer pricks. Instead, we were surrounded by about a dozen warriors in identical drab gray armor. Next to us in the center stood a couple of clerics. Nice mini-raid.

"These mannequins belong to you?" I asked.

Straad said, "They're all employees using an illusion clicky, so we look identical. The spooks insisted they be able to easily identify employees near the crime scene." With a shimmer, he activated his own character illusion. Now, he looked like a drab gray warrior as well.

Spooks?

"Crime scene," Alphadog nodded approval. "'Bout time."

I said, "Now we're talking. Let's get to work." The raid faced us. The whole scene was creepy, especially after I noticed what they were all doing.

All the cookie-cutter players were staring at Alpha. While they all appeared male in their illusionary form, it was a good bet some of them weren't. And they were not staring at Kelly, I reminded myself. Alphadog was a character in a game. No need to be jealous.

Never one to shy from a spotlight, she pivoted to face the group like a dancer on a stage, giving me a good view of her backside, which wasn't covered by the furry chaps. The game didn't allow a player to be completely nude, so all character models had built-in underwear, but damn.

I IM'ed her, "You can change back if you like. You're

being a scurvy elephant."

Kelly's sister had an eight-year-old daughter back on Earth. The story was that she had come home from school one day, saying that her teacher had called her a scurvy elephant. Naturally, her sister went to speak with the teacher, who revealed that her daughter was a *disturbing element* in class. In that context, Kelly was as scurvy as they come.

She messaged back, *"No need. It's starting to grow on me."*

I dropped the issue. Now that she knew I wanted her to change back, she would wear the crazy armor just to get a point over on me.

"Hey, don't we need the illusion, too?" I asked hopefully.

Straad shook his head, "No. You aren't employees."

It was worth a shot. Good thing Straad and I weren't competing, because I was losing. He seemed awfully experienced at saying no. Players probably bombarded him with requests all the time. Being a GM must not be all fun and games.

"Follow me," Straad said, walking off straight into the main tunnel.

I shouldn't have worried about getting bit by a bat. The mini-raid set up a perimeter around us, heavy on the leading edge. No mobs were in sight, but as we moved deeper into the tunnels, Shrieking Bats swooped down from the rough ceiling. The group's skillset belied their appearance. The illusion spell made them look like simple tanks, but they fought like every class in the game.

Shriekers were systematically mesmerized, nuked, shot, and backstabbed with impressive skill. The second someone was bitten, one of the clerics was dropping a complete heal like clockwork while another gave them a shot of cure disease in case they picked up bat fever. These guys were good.

"You know," I said, switching to the open channel. "Any time you guys form up a pick-up raid, send me a tell. Might be fun."

"They can't hear you," said Straad. "Orders are to stay in raid chat only. Everything else is blocked. They can't receive server-wide channels right now. Can't even take a screenshot."

"Orders from who?" Alphadog murmured.

We moved on, much deeper now than I had ever been in this zone. The remote-controlled rovers on Mars must be combing these tunnels like crazy, uploading their scans into International Space Agency mainframes for automated distribution to the public and the game. It was fascinating. These tunnels were not made by humans, or if they were, they weren't humans from Earth. The walls were strangely textured, like someone with a chainsaw making an ice sculpture. Players had tagged every clear spot with spray paint during the anniversary, even this deep into the passageways. Fortunately, it was just a digital overlay within the game. The real tunnels out on Mars would remain pristine, other than the rover traffic.

"Orders?" Alphadog asked, louder, when the GM hadn't responded. "Spooks? What kind of agents are we talking about?

ISA?"

"I really don't know," he said. "NSA, maybe. The only agent I'm allowed to talk to said his name's Jim Smith. Like that's a real name."

Alphadog snorted. "You probably don't know *my* real name, and I'm just FBI."

The gray men stopped in the middle of a six-way intersection, going into a defensive formation.

"Looks like a named bat just popped," said Alphadog. "Squalter and eight minions in a cove to the northwest."

Straad turned to me, "I don't know why you want to be a GM. You can already do most of what I can. Maybe we can talk later about your game plugins? We designed Squalter as a visual-only encounter. You're not supposed to be able to track her. Hell, I can't even see her on my GM map, though I can see that she's on the zone spawn list."

"That's," I hesitated, "not my department. I have no idea how it works. Mind if I join in the fight?"

"By all means, we shouldn't wipe, and there're two clerics for rez," Straad said. "Just keep in mind all your temp gear gets deleted if you die. I'm a Technovamp GM, not a candy store."

The encounter only took about five minutes. One player named Grin served as the tank, holding aggro on Squalter, while a couple of mystic types kept several of the minions mesmerized until the group was ready to tackle them. Most of the players dished out ranged DPS, except for one rogue who snuck around behind the current target assist for double-damage backstabs. I hate feeling useless, so I stayed at the rear of the group and lobbed grenades, taking care not to wake up the mezzed mobs. My sniper rifle tended to grab aggro, so I left it alone. I couldn't afford to lose the GM gear right now by dying.

After the named collapsed in a dramatic death screech, I waited to see if it dropped any good loot. Named mobs were uncommon, and usually dropped several nice items. "Who's looting?"

Straad didn't answer, but I saw an indicator on my status panel showing I had just been designated ML, Main Looter. I kneeled at the corpse of the ugliest bat I had ever seen. No way Kelly and I could have taken this brute out on our own, even with our augmented GM armor. I hit the loot hotkey and a list of items showed up in my loot window, which I linked to the group. Since I wasn't in the raid, only my group—Kelly and Straad— would get the list.

Kelly whistled, "Mostly vendor trash, but there's forty-two crystalline shards. That's a fortune!"

"No more than I can loot off the scouts in the Bloodfields after about twenty hours of soloing, but I'll take it." I paused. "Need or greed? Anybody want to roll for it?"

Straad responded, "Go for it. Don't delay. We were supposed to be there about five minutes ago."

"Um," I hated to say it. "My bags are full."

Straad approached. A trade window popped up containing a

sixty-slot backpack. I didn't hesitate to tap the Accept button and swapped it out with one of my wimpy twenty-slot bags, which I promptly dropped on the ground. I clicked loot-all and the new pack filled with shards and several random items. Named often dropped low-value quest items that you could use to obtain escalating rewards. I would sift through the other items later for anything useful.

After a few more minutes of running down the northwest tunnel, we exited into a large domed cavern. There wasn't as much graffiti this deep into the zone, but there were dozens of character names, rude comments, and vaguely sexual symbols. Alpha and I would never have been able to get here without a lot of help. All game creatures had been cleared, but I knew we would have to remain vigilant for repops.

The only objects in sight were randomly piled boulders, as if someone had been excavating. There were deep grooves crisscrossing the floor. Light was provided by dozens of will-o-the-wisps floating around the cavern. The place had that surprisingly bright-but-not-quite-sunlight feel of a professional sports arena. Off to the right, more gray men held a perimeter around a flat area, interspersed with a few nondescript male and female characters wearing black lab coats.

I asked Straad, "Are these mad scientists your mystery agents?"

"Yes, or at least that's what our CEO says," Straad seemed frustrated at being kept out of the loop. "All I know is I was told to give them whatever they asked for. You have no idea how much drama preceded your visit. The governor had to threaten to shut down the whole investigation if they didn't allow him to send in his own private team."

"We're the governor's private investigative team?" I was half impressed and half insulted. "I need to ask for a raise."

"Maybe he's not so evil after all," Alphadog said.

"Hold on a sec," something didn't feel right. "If this is a virtual world accessible from anywhere, then why does the governor of el Colorado have jurisdiction?"

I was asking Straad, but Alpha answered instead.

"The whole game is hosted at the same location as the primary Mars Rover program. It's a joint effort with a sharing of expenses. The game servers are right here in el Denver at the AHCCC. Literally upstairs from us. Don't you ever read the papers?"

"Yes, but any story that mentions the words 'high capacity computing' is your department. I keep my coding skills up, but you're way down in the weeds."

"True. That's why we make great partners."

As we approached the ring of players, one of the agents nodded and they parted to let us past the perimeter. As we passed, I brushed against the nearest lab coat and quipped, "What's the matter? Couldn't find any trench coats?"

There, in the center of the circle, was a player corpse. Someone had spray painted a crude chalky white outline around the body. "Did Kojak stop by to investigate?"

"No," Straad came up beside me, "but the group of players that first discovered the body had a similar sense of drama. Mostly kids. We interviewed them already, but they didn't know any more than what you can see for yourself. We've gotten criticism for allowing such vandalism of Mars, even virtual, but the paint fades over time. This time next week, the first of the paint will be fading."

I kneeled to examine the body more closely. It was wearing typical common armor from the game. The body resembled a human, short, thin, and had a helm that completely covered the face, making character identification difficult. The white body outline was sloppy, nicking the foot with a little overspray. It looked like a game corpse, except that there was no character name hovering above its head. I tried clicking on the corpse to target it but got nothing.

"I can't target it. Alpha do you see anything on your map?"

"No," she crouched next to me. "Player corpses despawn in one hour unless you get a rez first. Players in roleplay mode don't have a tag over their heads, but you should still be able to target them."

"We saw that, too," said Straad, crouching next to us. "Now we're here, I can speak freely, as it were. This morning I met with the devs. Their first assumption is that he or she is using some kind of illegal player stealth. A game plugin. They do exist. Their second assumption is that the character isn't actually dead, but the player is no longer animating it. In other words, the player is slumped in a cocoon, either unconscious or dead. Cocoons require constant unique health telemetry to keep a game character animated. That keeps players from physically controlling more than one character at a time. That would be cheating. If we didn't have that limitation, you could set up a hundred player clones and effectively solo any end-game raid target."

"How would that work?" I turned to look at Alpha. "Is there such a thing as that kind of stealth?"

"I figured you were about to ask that." Alphadog stood up and backed away from the corpse. "Let's do a test. Try to target me."

I tried but got no target. "I know I'm going to regret asking, but I need to understand this. How?"

"It's a simple matter of crafting IP packets outside the game. Easy with a well written app. Think of this. The game servers keep up with your location based on actions you take in your cocoon. They have little choice but to trust the cocoon to send the correct data, but they have strong data integrity controls. Things like check digits and CRC checksums."

"I knew I was going to regret it," I said. "Tone it down a notch. I need to understand, but I don't have time for a graduate course in game hacking."

Alphadog sighed. "You should really listen to me more often. Okay. If you fake the data, then the game knows immediately that you changed something. What you do is hack your pod with a plugin that intercepts the encrypted packet payload *after* it leaves the game engine. You disassemble it and then put it back together again with recalculated integrity codes. It's a man-in-the-middle exploit. That way, you can fool the server into thinking you're anywhere you want, while your local game client thinks you're somewhere else. You'd be a ghost, sort of. It confuses the servers. Remember where I was crouching next to you a second ago? I'm still there. Try and target me there."

Sure enough, I clicked the empty space next to me and Alphadog showed up in my targeting window. "You've been holding out on me. I could own this place with a plug-in like that."

"Restraint isn't one of your strong points. I'm not keeping secrets, just withholding temptation. My macros make things easier, but I never use one that lets you do things that are supposed to be impossible. Just because I can, doesn't mean that I do it. Besides, my whole life's work seems to be keeping you out of trouble."

"Enough lectures. I get it. Straad, did your devs look into that?"

"They did. We're aware of ghostkilling. Dozens of accounts have been perma-banned for it."

"I rest my case, detective," Alphadog crossed her arms.

"We locked down the zone right after the body was

discovered," Straad continued. "No one can get into the caves right now without a GM escort. We've been asking players to leave and port them elsewhere if they don't cooperate. We've systematically whittled players down to just the ones we know about. Anybody left on the zone spawn list other than us should be our victim."

Kelly interjected, "Then, once you nail down their IP address you can track their physical location. With the IP, you should be able to tap into their health and GPS telemetry. Case closed."

"Except," I said.

Straad nodded, "Except, we've accounted for every player on the zone list. This isn't regular ghosting."

I nodded. "If it were, we wouldn't be here."

"Right." Straad stood up. "I need to give the agents a status update. Call me if you need me." He walked a few steps, then stopped and turned around. "And go easy on the hacks. The last thing we need is to crash the game zone." He left.

I started putting together a plan. "Kelly, I need you to photograph the crime scene."

Alphadog shrugged. "Screenshots maybe?"

"Yes. Set your display to maximum resolution. Crouch down to simulate zoom."

"Do you know me at all? I got this."

"Okay," I nodded. "Just making sure. This is the first completely digital crime scene that I know of. It might be the first one in history. Start with the corpse from all angles, and then spiral out from there until you run out of time."

Kelly was already crouching over the body. "You think we'll run out of time? What's the hurry?"

"I'm not sure yet." I looked around the brightly lit cavern, then climbed onto a nearby pile of rubble topped with a large boulder. I slowly scanned the whole area before realizing I couldn't see the whole room.

"Kelly?"

"Hmm?"

She sounded distracted. I looked to see what she was doing. The first thing I noticed was that her outfit was back to its normal form-fitting look. "You changed."

"I know. The armor was getting in the way of the shots."

I nodded. It was easy to imagine two particular parts of the armor that might have been getting in the way of downward-facing screenshots. I didn't need her to draw a picture for me.

"Good," I nodded. "Our guide mentioned something about a clipping plane earlier."

"Yeah. It limits how far away things are rendered on your display. Things that are far away take up unnecessary processing power and are mostly irrelevant to game play."

"Making them effectively invisible. How do I see the whole cavern?"

"Game options, general tab, user interface, look for the clipping slider and push it all the way to the right."

I followed Kelly's instructions and could soon see the far wall. Two tiny agents at the far end seemed to be guarding a small tunnel opening. Thinking about what could be seen and what could not, I checked the game forums for additional information. It was time to earn my paycheck.

I sent a personal text to Alphadog, *"You have about 18 min to get your shots before the next map refresh. Make it count."*

Her answer was a simple, "Will do." We played around a lot, but when it counted, I had to acknowledge that Kelly was right. We made a hell of a team. I took off running across the cavern.

As I approached the agents, they positioned themselves to block the small tunnel opening. It was narrow and had a low ceiling. Standing close enough to get their full attention, I said, "I just need to ask you a question or two."

They glanced at each other. Both were large male warriors. The one on the left answered, "We're not authorized to answer any questions. Please return to the perimeter."

"Okay, whatever. Hold on a sec. I'm in 'tell hell' with all these text messages. Gotta let Agent Smith know what I'm doing over here. Straad is using all caps. Didn't mean to cause a commotion."

It was a flat out lie. I dug around in my inventory for the Eye of Zona I had purchased from the Customer Service vendors. It was a simple clicky, but I knew there would be a visible character animation from activating the item. There always was. I clicked the eye and then immediately tried to hide the casting by clicking the hotkey to load the same lingerie set I had triggered earlier. I figured there was a better than even chance they would both be distracted by my glistening gauze-covered body. I had to admit, Sleepkiller was a knockout in undies.

"Oh, sorry," I said. "So embarrassing. I really need to rearrange these hotkeys."

They didn't respond but kept a close eye on me. What I could see, but they couldn't, was a floating eyeball behind them in the mouth of the tunnel. Moments ago, I had looked up how to use the eye on player forums. I was rooted in place. Any movement I tried to make would now apply to the eyeball instead of my character, and what it saw was displayed in a picture-in-picture window. I quickly floated the Eye of Zona down the tunnel until it reached a tee intersection. The way was obvious, since the right tunnel was brightly lit. Rounding the corner, I got the shock of my life.

The most beautiful sculpture I've ever seen sat on a pedestal. It was like a hippopotamus, but with three horns and a flared bony plate across the back of its neck. It must be some sort of a triceratops. A dinosaur, but typical artist renderings that I had seen underestimated the muscle mass by half. The figure was incredibly strong looking, bulging like an Olympic weightlifter. Bristly hairs that almost reminded me of feathers covered its body. It was pitch black, with golden eyes. The closer

I looked, the more I could make out intricate patterns in its spiky fur.

One lab-coated agent levitated above the ground, peering into the dino's eyeballs. A second one crouched at the base, which was covered with what my untrained eye saw as Greek letters. I could recognize pi, as well as the one that looked like an upside down 'y.' I grabbed a screenshot and then killed the Eye of Zona.

Now that I was no longer rooted, I hotkeyed my standard armor back into place. "Sorry for the misunderstanding. I'll leave you to whatever it is you do here." I ran.

Neither of the agents down the small tunnel at the statue had been looking in my direction, but someone must have noticed something. Straad intercepted me coming through the perimeter.

"What did you do!"

"I was just surveilling like I was supposed to do."

Another agent broke through from the opposite direction, a female character model with long white hair. She had a female voice as well. "You were supposed to track down the body in the real world, not wander off in the game. Give me one reason I shouldn't arrest you this minute."

"Because," I checked the time. "Because I just solved the mystery of the digital corpse."

"This had better be good," the agent didn't sound like one used to being thwarted. "What have you found." It sounded more like an accusation than a question.

"You're Agent Smith, right?"

"My name is about to become your worst nightmare. Start talking."

"Somehow, I don't think you're really interested in the body." I left the implied question hanging until I got bored waiting. I wasn't known for my patience. "Why are you here?"

"I'm the one asking the questions. Talk."

If there's one thing I hated, it was government employees who didn't like answering my questions.

"I'm fairly sure, though it's possible I'm wrong, that you are about to lose your corpse and your crime scene for good. I hope you took a lot of pictures."

Agent Smith responded, "I have agents on the moon. Whatever you saw, I have your ass on that NDA and a federal prosecutor on speed-dial. You'll keep your mouth shut."

"I doubt that," but I wasn't sure. It took all my self-control to keep from glancing at Kelly. I did have a lot to lose, and I had a feeling that the agent did as well.

Several more agents entered the circle from all directions, guns raised and aimed straight at me.

"What're you going to do? Kill my character? Newsflash, that'll only send me back to my bind point, which isn't here." I spun in place, both impressed and alarmed by the thick circle of intermingled agents and GMs surrounding us.

Agent Smith motioned downward. Everyone lowered their rifles, swords, staffs, and every type of science-fantasy weapon in the game. "They'll be at your physical location in minutes. Whatever you think you saw in that tunnel, I have your ass on that NDA and if I don't get a damn good explanation right now, you'll be stepping out of your cocoon into handcuffs."

"Okay, chill." I looked around until I spotted Alphadog, wishing I could see her real-world face. She was standing up, watching the proceedings, no longer taking screen shots. I had no idea how they detected my snooping. The Eye of Zona was supposed to be invisible to everyone but the caster. "Everything will be just fine. I came here for a reason, and I can deliver."

I walked slowly toward the fallen player, keeping my eye on the time. Opening my character inventory, I found one of the spray cans I had purchased earlier. I chose the pink one. It was Kelly's favorite color. Crouching down next to the corpse, I promptly spray-painted a hot pink 'X' across the corpse's chest.

"Hey!" Agent Smith yelled. "Why did you do that? This is a crime scene. That's obscuring evidence. Get her out of here. And get that spray can."

"Geeze, hold off a second. This is instructive, not destructive." I stood and faced her. "I'm answering your question. There are plenty of good theories going around, but by the time I get involved it usually isn't any of the obvious ones. Based on the evidence," I was interrupted by a chime that resounded throughout the entire game. It was right on time. "Based on the evidence, your corpse," My screen, indeed every screen in the game, dissolved to black and then reloaded. "Your corpse is not here."

At my feet, the corpse was gone. My "X" was exactly where I had left it, hovering over the floor.

"Can I arrest you now?" Agent Smith's voice dripped with sarcasm. "Are you done screwing around with my investigation? I have people who can figure out whatever hack it is you just did. I should never have allowed you on site." She put fists on her hips, "Damn civilians."

Straad shook his head. "I get it. I should have realized."

"Realized what?" asked Agent Smith.

"Your corpse is not a player," I answered, "or even in the game. Your corpse is on Mars."

The entire group was silent, waiting to see what the agent-in-charge would say.

When she answered, her voice was even, monotone, and the words came slowly. "There are no corpses on Mars. There are no people on Mars. If there were, I would know. There haven't been any manned missions to Mars in over a decade."

Straad answered, a bit hesitantly. "I'm afraid I have to disagree. The servers just loaded the latest Rover scans. It's very nearly indisputable."

While I appreciated the support, I didn't want Straad stealing every bit of thunder. I quickly interjected. "The first thing you might have noticed is the faint spatter of paint on the victim's shoe. In game, the spray paint sticks to the environment, but not the players, and that would include player corpses." I knew I had worded it with a slight dig at what the professional agents might or might not have noticed, but I decided my conscience could live with it.

"We—might've—noticed that. I didn't realize the hoodlums couldn't tag each other. Someone didn't do a very thorough briefing." The last three words came out with jagged edges in her voice. Agent Smith looked pointedly at Technovamp Straad.

Poor Straad looked shaken. It's good to be the GM. Playing a game for a living? That's a tough job to lose.

An employment offer like that might entice me to give up being a detective. On the other hand, I was glad to learn that I wasn't the only one scared shitless by these no-agency agents.

Standing precariously on top of the painted "X," which I found to be just as solid as the cavern floor, I continued. "The rovers were swarming all over the unnatural cavern photographing everything in response to a motivated public. Scientists, theologians, gamers, basically every human alive was captivated by the revelation of carved tunnels on another planet."

"Then something happened on Mars, in the real tunnels. The cameras stumbled upon a dead body and dutifully digitized it from every angle as a new object. Not only is your body on the red planet, but sometime in the last twenty-four hours, your murderer disposed of the corpse. That's what I was betting on while waiting for the mainframes to boot up the new zone map. My little trip across the cavern was as much killing time as being snoopy. I didn't really expect to find proof of highly advanced aliens, maybe even ancient humans, down your little side tunnel. This whole cavern probably had artifacts all over it at some point, and whoever's still living on Mars wanted to keep them a secret."

That's when it all became clear. I had just drawn a card to the inside of a royal flush. "I wonder if the body isn't a fake. It would make a great distraction for someone who needs more time to excavate, to get rid of whatever evidence." Bringing up a window to our evidence drive, I looked at Kelly's screenshots from before the corpse disappeared. "Just the way I remembered it. The leggings the corpse was wearing are supposed to tuck into the boots, but they come down too far, like the pants were made for someone a little taller than our player, or," I paused for effect, "we have what amounts to a short mannequin dressed like a player."

Straad touched his forehead. "I saw that. I even mentioned to the developers last night that their textures weren't lining up right on the Sylvan armor set. It never occurred to me this set was essentially a photograph of real armor on a real person. It wasn't generated by the game. It was real armor. Or cosplay armor, in any case. Someone did quite the job casting those."

My paranoia downshifted into the straightaway, most likely speeding me back into another jail cell, fueled by anger as much as the fear of what they could do to me. To both of us. I was flying into a danger zone, but I didn't care. Hopefully, Kelly would understand. I hoped she wouldn't lose her job, because I was pretty sure I was already way beyond any parole violation. I didn't like being mocked.

I stepped toward Agent Smith and stopped, poking a finger at her face. "You brought me here to fail. That's why you're really here, isn't it? Was that even a corpse? Maybe it was just some kind of movie prop thrown down by your shady little agency as a distraction. Your real objective was to get the company to shut down this game zone so players wouldn't discover what you're really up to. This is a coverup."

Running up on top of the boulder pile again, I pointed to the nearby piles of rubble and boulders, and to the grooves in the floor, "Somebody's been excavating here, extracting secrets from this cavern. You didn't want the public to see it. What was it? Aliens, humans, dinosaurs?" I jumped down and confronted Agent Smith. She had a shocked expression. "Whatever your cloak-and-dagger maneuver is, the rovers swarmed in here too fast, didn't they? The game would reveal too much, too soon, to the public. It would be suspicious if they started malfunctioning all of a sudden. So you did the next best thing. Shut out the players. Lower your crooked little veil of secrecy and threaten anyone who doesn't play your version of the game. The only crime here is you."

I knew I was right. The look on Agent Smith's face told me she was buying it. Unfortunately, unless she was a brilliant actress, the revelation was new to her. The next expression confirmed it. Agent Smith's jaw hardened, and her fingers clenched the air. I suspected in the real world, her face was turning red. She had been playing me for a fool, but someone else had been playing her first.

I hate to think of myself as a drama queen, but if the show fits. Maybe I'd get lucky and they'd give me my own episode on the History channel; Infamous detective goes missing in alien cyberspace.

I held out my wrists, bowed my head, and announced, "You may arrest me now."

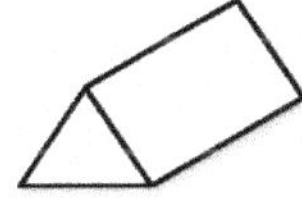

Fortunately, they didn't.

Instead, after debriefings that lasted longer than the whole investigation had taken, the governor sprung for a night in the best hotel in the city. Once I had the room key, I pointed out to Mayor Sheldon the clause in our contract regarding a standing minimum fee. This had to be my shortest investigation ever and I wasn't about to settle for half a day's pay.

The room wasn't like anything in el Vegas, but not too shabby. It was twice the size of our place back home, and had a large window overlooking el Denver. Almost all sleeping areas on the moon are underground to block the solar radiation, so it was a treat to stand in my nightgown—a real one this time, on my real body—and look out at the stars. I let the view soak in. Three stories below, a mining truck returned from the rare earth mines on the other side of the crater. Miners in suits poured out the door and jumped off the roof before it even came to a stop.

Kelly took my hand, distracting me from the view by giving me a better one. She was in a filmy wrap far skimpier than my nightgown. An aroma washed over me. The scent was one part carnival cotton candy and one part sunset over the Rocky Mountains. She had a perfume like no other, or a mixture of things that I had never figured out. Not that I was any expert.

"I saw something out there," I said. "Something important. And they confiscated it all. My proof is in the hands of someone I can't even name. My console, my camera, my drives. That's a business expense. The mayor's going to buy me new stuff, and we only spent, what, maybe five hours start to finish? Can't pay my rent with that."

"I know."

"You didn't see it."

"The statue? Two guys looking it over?"

I held her at arm's length to get a good look at her face. "You didn't see what I saw." Her words were still sinking in. I hadn't told her about the two scientist agents. "How?"

"You didn't think I was too busy to keep track of you, 'cause I'll never be too busy for that. Somebody's got to watch your back, little felon. You could trip over a moon rock and somehow end up behind bars for it. As soon as I saw two agents chasing you back to the corpse, I put myself in ghost mode, yanked my harness, and did a backup of everything back at the computer center."

I wondered where my breath had gone. "All of it?"

She slipped into her best mischievous smile. "Crime scene photos from my pod, statue photos from yours. I ran a streaming copy of everything we both saw, the whole trip." She nodded. "Every face we saw, every groove on the crater floor, and every word spoken. I was doing a hell of a lot more than taking snapshots of a corpse."

"Didn't Fender try to stop you?" I asked.

Kelly said, "She was in one of the pods, logged into the game, but I only had a few minutes before the agents showed up."

"But they confiscated and searched everything. It was all wiped." I was bewildered. Those assholes didn't leave anything to chance. "I don't know about you, but they checked everything. The bastards touched me in ways that I barely allow you to do."

"They didn't do everything. No MRI. No X-Rays." She gave me her best innocent look. "You'll have the goods in about a day and a half."

I just nodded. Kelly could be brash, even a bit of an exhibitionist at times, but there were a few personal activities that she preferred to keep private. Instead, I drew her in, wrapping around her, touching everything in reach with everything I had from neck to ankles. I tightened when she exhaled until I could feel every breath, until I could feel her heart beating.

My chest tightened. I felt dizzy. Wordlessly, she loosened my hold and led me to the overstuffed couch, pushing me down into the cushions. My legs parted as we intertwined, her soft body filling me with tremors of sensuality as she pressed into mine.

My lips found hers even with my eyes closed, coming home to rest, it seemed. Our lips parted from the outset, I rediscovered the faint ridge of scar tissue along the right side of her tongue, reportedly from too many rounds of self-defense practice. The underside of her tongue and below was as soft as her breasts conforming to my own, driving me crazy.

I surged urgently upward with my knee. Kelly accommodated, but wasn't going to let me rush it. Around and around we floated in a sea of warmth, of slick wetness, and a faint taste of salt. The first few minutes, it was hard to breathe. The pounding of my heart drove my lungs to crave more oxygen. I needed air, panting every other wave as we rocked against each other. Our lips never stopped touching.

As my heartbeat steadied, our practiced rhythm took over. I pulled my tongue in, and she retreated far enough not to get bit. It's hard to swallow without bringing your teeth together, and I had the saliva of two. It was the briefest of motions, not even interrupting our steady roll into the abyss. I repeated the dance until I lost count, restarting the pulse of our bodies beating together like a single heart.

I had no idea how long we had been together, but suddenly I

came back into myself as though I had been on a journey far from my own body. My arms were mine again, and a thrill of desire swept through me. God she was the best thing that had ever happened to me.

Our phones rang.

"Mmm," I broke off the kiss. "That only happens on TV shows, right?"

Kelly whispered, "That's the ring for the business line."

I nodded, reluctantly, almost imperceptibly. "Might be a paying customer."

The pressure across me eased, cool air drying our sweat, leaving me tingling in regret. This was not over, but the momentum was gone. We might have to start all over again. That wouldn't be altogether a bad thing. We hadn't even tried out the bed yet. In an expensive hotel like this, the mattress was bound to feel like cuddling puppies. Moon mattresses could afford to be softer and still provide support in low moon gravity.

Kelly had answered, already listening intently. By her expression, it had to be important.

Covering the mouthpiece, she said, "It's Takoda Onebird. On an encrypted line."

I sat up so fast my head spun. Either that or it was still spinning from before. "UNOOSA?" The chill of evaporating sweat turned to goosebumps.

Kelly nodded, still listening. She started spelling our last names and reciting our social security numbers. After that, it was some kind of FBI mumbo jumbo that only bureaucrats could dream up. She mentioned a transference of jurisdiction, but I was already tuning it out.

This was like getting a call from Fox Mulder. Takoda was a Native American that headed up the Office of Outer Space Affairs for the United Nations. I had his autograph on a printed program from a space travel symposium I had attended back on Earth. How could he know what we had done? And so soon?

After a while my curiosity couldn't take any more. I mouthed silently, "What does he want?"

She held a hand up, clearly listening to some important detail. Her eyes met mine with a twinkle that could only mean I would like what she was about to say.

"Jaz's time starts at liftoff," she said into the phone. "Because her consulting business has to be put on hold, and we'll both be on standard government per diem."

My tablet chimed with an incoming message.

Kelly paused, covering the phone again and motioning toward my tablet, "You have some paperwork to fill out for an interim clearance. And he wants to know if your passport is up to date."

"My what?" The answer was obvious. We were on the Moon. You couldn't get here without a valid passport. "I mean, of course it is."

Tumblers fell into place. It was too good to be true. The UN had either intercepted an intelligence report coming from Agent

Smith, or she had been working for UNOOSA all along.

"Of course, we'd be glad to pursue the matter further," another pause. "Yes, I'll contact the administrative office in the morning." Kelly sat the phone down.

"So?" I asked, hardly daring to believe what I thought was about to happen.

"Think you're up to a special assignment? We would be gone a long time. They've decided to send a team to investigate your findings."

"We're the team?"

Kelly nodded. "Part of it."

"My probation?"

"Pardoned, most likely. Either way, I'd be the special agent in charge. I can grant you a special dispensation for your parole restrictions if necessary, with a little help from a federal judge."

"To Mars?"

"To wherever the investigation might lead," she nodded, "starting with Mars."

I jumped up and squealed, a sound I don't think I've ever made before. I ran up, grabbed Kelly's hand, and took off running. The two of us ran through the double doorway into the bedroom and leaped into cuddly puppies together.

I could fill out that paperwork tomorrow. A girl had to have her priorities.

Erik Johnson

Erik Johnson is a retired engineer and had a varied career from replacing iron telephone wires across the rural Wyoming landscape to construction projects at secret military sites around the world. His third career is now fiction writing and putting a notebook full of what-if scenarios into stories. He currently lives in Colorado with four cats and a room filled with books and a writing desk.

Gwendolyn Isn't a Lizard

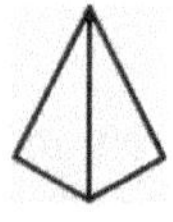

Fantasy Humor

By

Erik Johnson

Len welcomed the crunch of tires on the gravel driveway. He glanced at the clock hanging under the cupboard for the hundredth time and smiled. Deb came in and threw her bulging backpack onto the couch. She swept back blonde bangs and headed straight to the fridge and pulled out a soda.

"Where've you been, kid? I expected you two hours ago."

She dropped into an easy chair and propped her feet on the coffee table. "Stopped at Hamburger City for a bite and ran into a few friends."

"I assumed you'd come straight home from Crested Butte. So, how was the summer college prep art camp?"

Deb flipped back her blonde ponytail. "It was great. I learned to draw horses like a pro in a session called Life with a Pencil."

"That's nice, but have any fun?"

"Sure did." She drained the soda can. "Plenty of cute guys, but I was too busy to go out on dates."

Len shook his head and went to the coffee maker. "Did you keep them away with a big stick?"

"I really tried, but my arms got so tired, and then I—"

Len slapped her shoulder and frowned before smiling.

"I'll tell you everything after supper, so what have you been doing?" she asked.

"You told me to stop bringing work home, but—" Len turned at the sound of the bed squeaking in the bedroom.

"What was that?" She turned her head.

"Probably Gwendolyn," He answered.

"Oh, got a roommate with benefits?" Deb gave him a wry smile.

"Not exactly."

The bedroom door creaked open a crack, then a blue feather-covered nose nudged it wide open. A 5-foot tall monster, balancing on two muscular legs ending in claws, stopped for a moment before clicking across the floor to Deb.

A look of horror filled Deb's eyes as Gwendolyn stopped, inches away and looked at her with unblinking yellow eyes. Deb gasped and squirmed away.

"Relax and meet my new pet, Gwendolyn. I got her last month, so Gwen, say hello to my daughter, Deborah."

The creature took a step back, balancing on bird-like feet, and whipped her long tail. She tilted her head, eyebrows lifted into a curious expression, and her jaw eased open to display razor sharp white teeth.

"A lizard covered with blue feathers, what the hell is this thing?"

Len held out his arm and Gwendolyn scurried over to shove her head under his hand. "Gwen isn't a lizard. She's a Velociraptor."

Deb stood. "You're insane. Nobody has a Velociraptor."

"I do."

"This thing is a cold-blooded killer, not a house pet."

He rubbed Gwendolyn under the chin. "More like an oversized kitten. Have to keep her fed, or the fun goes away."

She looked at Gwendolyn, and Gwendolyn looked at her.

Neither moved as Len spoke, "Gwen, the ball."

Gwendolyn ran back into the bedroom, her claws clicking on the wood floor.

"She'll be back in a minute." Len put hands on his hips. "She better not break the--"

A crash broke his words.

"new bed lamp." He sighed and raised his palms in frustration.

Gwendolyn bounded into the living room and dropped a grapefruit-sized wooden ball at Len's foot. He picked up the ball and held it out to Deb. She slipped a finger into a deep gouge.

"Her favorite toy, but they don't last long," Len said, bouncing it in his palm. "Watch this."

Gwendolyn Isn't a Lizard

He lofted the ball down the hallway, and Gwendolyn leaped spinning into the air. She landed halfway across the living room at a dead run and disappeared into the hallway. She came back shaking her head with the ball tight between her teeth. The ball clattered to the floor, and Len grabbed it for another toss. Gwendolyn shifted from one foot to the other and a large sickle-shaped claw between two toes tapped the floor in anticipation. After a dozen pitches, she took slow steps to a steel water bowl by the fridge. Four wolves lapping up water couldn't make as much noise.

"Someone re-sequenced the most dangerous creature on the planet, and you have one running around the house? You've totally lost it, and I'm out of here." She started to rise.

Len pulled her back down. "No, don't go. Let me explain."

She pursed her lips and frowned.

"In July I worked at the Bio-Gen Industries lab in Denver repairing DNA matrix emulators. One day a mother hatched an egg but abandoned it. I wasn't busy so I helped them out by cradling the newborn and dropping chunks of goat meat into her mouth. I have all my fingers, so it worked. She must think I'm her mother. They were ready to put her down. Everyone thought she could become far too dangerous to keep around, but I begged and pleaded to get custody."

Gwendolyn sat next to Deb making muffled pert sounds and rested a front claw on Deb's leg. Deb turned to Len with a quizzical expression. "What's she doing?"

He went to the kitchen counter and looked over his shoulder. "She wants to be petted, so go ahead. Stroke above her eyebrows. She really likes that."

Deb ran her hand over Gwen's forehead and down the back of her neck.

Gwendolyn closed her eyes and scooted closer. Another stroke and Gwendolyn relaxed with soft deep gurgles.

"She doesn't smell like a cat or a dog. It reminds me of a rain-soaked sleeping bag."

"You sure have the touch. Gwen doesn't do that for me." Len turned around and scooped fresh grounds into the coffee machine.

When Deb stopped and pulled back her hand, Gwendolyn put both forearms on her knee and looked up.

Deb stroked narrow blue feathers on the side of Gwen's face and the gurgles got louder. "How long does she expect me to do this?"

Len squinted at the ceiling. "Oh, twelve hours should do it."

She dropped her hand, and Gwendolyn nudged her nose under it. "What if I stop right now?"

Len tapped a button and the red brewing light came on. "Eating your arm is her way of telling you to keep petting." He walked over and dropped into a well-worn easy chair and reached to stroke Gwen's back.

A look of horror filled Deb's eyes and she pulled her hand away.

"Just kidding. She's pretty much a cross between a puppy and a kitten with a touch of horse. Very intelligent and responds to voice commands. Watch this." Len crossed his arms. "Gwen, go outside."

Gwendolyn spun and bounded to the back door. She raised onto tiptoes and grasped the door handle. A quick pull opened the door, and she disappeared.

"Replaced the doorknob with a handle. Gwen can twist one, but a handle is much easier."

Deb leaned across the sink to look out the window. "She's chasing the horses. Will she eat them?"

"No, they get along and run around the pasture together. It was rather tense the first few days. I kept Gwen in a metal bar enclosure loaned by the lab. They bumped noses a few times, so I took a chance and let Gwen run free. That reminds me. I need to go to town and get more Gwen food. Want to come?"

A horse chased Gwendolyn around the tool shed, and Deb shook her head. "I suppose so. Where are we going?"

Len opened the back door and whistled. He stepped aside as Gwendolyn ran in. "Dave's Meat Market on First Street. He saves scraps and bones for me. He likes Gwen."

Len stepped out the front door and pointed to his pickup parked in the driveway. Gwen scampered to the passenger door and bounced up and down. Deb jerked the door open and pieces of seat padding fell on her shoes.

"Gwen's hard on truck upholstery, so I need to get the seat

fixed. Dave says I should make one from cast iron. Sit in the middle because Gwen likes to ride with her head out the window."

Deb slid in and Gwendolyn hopped onto the torn seat next to her. Her tail slapped across Len's face as he climbed in, knocking off his glasses. She licked his ear before turning toward Deb. Len retrieved his glasses and slid them on as Gwendolyn pushed her nose under Deb's chin.

"Reach across and pull the door shut." He turned the ignition key.

Len's right hand draped over the steering wheel and his left elbow rested on the door against the half open window as they pulled into town. Gwendolyn's neck stretched forward, and her chin rested on the side mirror. Her tail rested on Deb's legs and the tip swung back and forth between Len's chest and the steering wheel. When they stopped, a terrified elderly driver next to them frantically rolled up her driver's window and then sped away through a red light.

Deb spit out a small blue feather. "She's not the most popular pet in Woodland Park, is she?"

Len turned into Dave's Meat Market's empty parking lot and stopped at the front door. "Oh, it varies. Kids love Gwen, and I take her to the city park on Saturday afternoons for a petting session. At first the parents weren't very happy, but it's okay now. The Pattersons in Pine Canyon are raising a Stegosaurus, and the kids love him, too. Unfortunately, he's a growing boy and it will take a flatbed truck to haul him around next summer. You should see their hay bill."

Deb laughed and rubbed Gwendolyn under the chin as Len got out.

Len stared at a scrawled 'closed' sign taped to the front door and leaned forward to read the small print.

"What is it?"

He climbed back in and crossed arms over the steering wheel. "Dave is a volunteer deputy sheriff and is part of the manhunt. The sign says a man held up the credit union and shot a teller. Law enforcement is combing the hills looking for him." He dropped his chin to his arms. "He'll be back sometime Monday, but Gwen's food will only last into Saturday. No trip into town to play with the kiddies, and I don't want to lose another goat."

"What'll you do now?"

He leaned back. "Meat at the grocery store is too expensive, and Gwen has a healthy appetite for sirloin steaks. It'll break the bank, but I have no other choice. She also likes Hamburger City Double Deckers, but it would take ten each mealtime to fill her. For dessert it's dried peaches I get at the natural food store.

Len stroked a claw as Gwendolyn curled her tail across her own tucked legs. "Colorado Game and Fish says we have too many deer this year, so, I anticipate an open hunting season."

Deb's eyes lit up. "Why not go up to Tarryall Reservoir and let Gwendolyn do the hunting? Bring back what she doesn't mangle."

Len smiled. "I knew you were smarter than the average bear. That's a great idea. She's never hunted in the wild. This'll be quite a learning experience. The bio-genetics people check in every week to see how she's doing, and one of them said she's a natural hunter. Gwen needs to learn the ways of our post-Cretaceous Period world."

The quiet drive through Woodland Park was uneventful, and drivers going the other way didn't seem to notice a blue head sticking out the window. He pulled off the narrow dirt road leading to the reservoir and stopped at an open area between the pine trees. They got out and Gwendolyn took off at a dead run and disappeared. Len put his back to the headlights and crossed his arms. "We might be here for a while."

Late morning stretched into afternoon, and Deb dropped her elbows to the hood. "What's she doing?"

"No idea." Len cupped hands over his eyes and scanned the trees. "I don't want to wait here all day, so let's go find her."

"Suppose she got a deer?"

Len pointed to a narrow trail disappearing into the trees. "She's had time to get two or three of them. Let's go this way. I hear crashing sounds, so probably Gwen."

The narrow trail twisted around rock outcroppings and into thickening underbrush as they approached a stream. Water splashing over round rocks was the only sound.

"Will she come if you whistle?" Deb asked, struggling to catch her breath.

"Usually, but I don't know if she's close enough to hear. Damned lizard."

"You told me Gwendolyn isn't a lizard."

"She is today." Len took a deep breath and screamed, "Gwen! Dinner."

"It isn't dinner time."

"No, but she knows that word and will come at top speed."

Len was ready to shout again when a tall man with a scarred face and fierce eyes stepped from behind a rock. He shoved a pistol barrel into Len's face. "Far enough."

Len fell back next to Deb and raised his arms. "Oh, shit. I don't have a gun."

The man scowled and cocked the hammer. "Too bad. I do."

"We're only looking for Gwen."

"I'll get Gwen but first I'll deal with you two. Can't have no witnesses, cops are too close." He narrowed his eyes. "I'll start with missy."

He pointed the pistol at Deb's forehead, and Len lowered his arms.

"Gwen, dinner."

The man turned around at the sound of cracking twigs, and a blue blur with two extended sickle claws landed on his face.

Deb turned away from Gwen crunching bones.

Gwendolyn stood on the corpse, lowered her neck and lifted one leg. She let out a low roar like a lion ready to attack.

"Do you know what this means?" Len asked.

Deb bent over with hands on her knees and threw up. "No, I don't."

"It means I don't have to buy a home burglar alarm system."

A.M. Burns

A.M. Burns lives in the Colorado Rockies with his partner, several dogs, cats, horses, and birds. When he's not writing, he's often fixing fences, splitting wood, hiking in the mountains, or flying his hawks. He's enjoyed writing since he was in high school, but it wasn't until the past few years that he's begun truly honing his craft. He is a previous president of the Colorado Springs Fiction Writers Group: www.csfwg.org. Having lived both in Colorado and Texas, rugged frontier types and independent attitudes often show up in his work.

Enter the Spellslinger

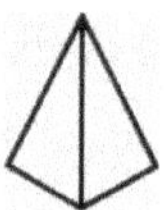

Weird Western Heist

by

A.M. Burns

It was nearly sunset. Ezra Vyxon had his storse pushed to its fastest. Its heavy metal hooves kicked up a constant plume of dust that mingled with the construct's steam as they crossed the dusty eastern Colorado plains and followed the Arkansas River toward Pueblo. He stayed just off the green belt the river created to give the mechanical steed better traction and increased speed.

The message said to meet at sunset at a saloon on the eastern side of Pueblo. He hoped he would make it. If he hadn't run into a pack of werewolves attacking a stagecoach a few miles west of La Junta, it wouldn't have been a problem, but he wasn't about to leave innocent people to a nasty fate when there was something he could do about it.

Ezra wished he could create a portal and ride through it, but one drawback to the storse was its metal body would disrupt the portal, and he wouldn't be able to control where he came out. Odds were he could end up farther from his destination than he already was. He kept watching the sky and hoped he wouldn't be the last one to arrive. He hated being late, even if he did have a good story to explain his tardiness. By the time they reached Pueblo, he'd had to turn on the storse's eye lights to be able to see the trail. There weren't a lot of businesses on the east side of town. The stockyards were there, and most proprietors liked places a little less smelly, and a little quieter, but the Silver Spur Saloon did a good business with the cowboys, so it worked well for them. Ezra pulled the storse to a stop outside the saloon where others had tied their horses to the hitching posts. He didn't bother tying the storse; being a steam construct, it would stay until he mounted again and started its engine, that was as much steam as magic.

Light spilled out the windows and doors of the saloon, and from the sounds and number of horses, the place was already packed to the rafters. Based on the well-trampled ground along the banks, Ezra surmised that a large herd had recently been driven along the river and reached Pueblo.

When Ezra entered the saloon, he paused a couple of steps beyond the doors. He scanned the room, trying to find the people he was meeting. It didn't take him long to spot a familiar, distinctive stove pipe hat.

Ezra entered the fray and headed toward the hat as it bobbed through the throng to the bar. "Jefferson, you old sod," he said as he walked up to the bar.

"Ah, Ezra, I was beginning to think you'd been waylaid or something, but Bloodclaw said you'd be late." Jefferson picked up the four beers the bartender had set on the bar, his large hands easily carrying the beverages. "One more for my friend here."

"Thanks." Ezra picked up the fifth beer. "Where is everyone else?"

"Far corner. Sly got here early and figured with the cows coming in the place would fill up early, so he staked us out a table."

"So, Sly's here too." Ezra kept his feelings about the seer out of his tone. He could work with Sly Turner, but he'd never let the man ride behind him. He didn't trust the bastard that much. He made a point to never make the same mistake twice, and Sly Turner was always a mistake. "Mac's message didn't say who would be here, just that he was getting a posse together for an important job."

Jefferson laughed as they cut through the crowd. Most people tended to get out of the big man's way, even if a lot of his perceived size was due to the hat and the huge curved sword slung over his back. It was a good idea to not get in Jefferson Tarrant's way. "A posse? He called us a posse. Not sure what he wants us to do, could be considered saving people."

They got close enough to the table, and Ezra recognized everyone sitting there. Bloodclaw was one of the biggest Sioux he'd ever met, one of the biggest men, period. His long black braids draped down the front of his flak vest that had been carved to look like a native battle vest. Sly Turner was still obviously sly, looking a little too polished for a saloon just outside a stockyard. His blond hair was slicked back and cut shorter than the last time Ezra had seen him, but he still had it long enough to braid a couple of protective beads in it. Like most people who looked out of place in the saloon, he was good at manipulating people and pulling fast ones on them. Mac Goldthwaite was a small man, slender, short, looked like he could vanish into a crowd with no effort whatsoever, and had been known to do so on more than a few occasions. As he looked very average, clean shaven, with dark brown hair barely poking out of his bowler hat, people only noticed him when he wanted them to. He was a very powerful tinker, and when he called people to lend a hand, that meant it was something major, and something that would most likely prove to be profitable.

"You finally got here." Mac grinned as he took the beer Jefferson offered him.

"Just a little slow down." Ezra claimed the last open chair at the scratched up table.

"Most people wouldn't consider a pack of werewolves robbing a stagecoach a little slow down." Bloodclaw claimed his beer, then took a long drink.

"Good thing I'm not most people." Ezra set down his glass after his first sip. The beer was a lot weaker than he expected, even out on the edge of nowhere like Pueblo, Colorado.

Mac chuckled and downed half of his beer in one fast drink. "If you were most people, I wouldn't have called you in for help."

"Right." Jefferson took off his hat and scratched his head. "So, Mac, enlighten us as to why we're here."

"There's a vampire coming into the state, got some powerful magics with him that we need to relieve him of." Mac finished off his beer and set the glass on the table a little harder than necessary.

Jefferson frowned. "Robbing a vampire? Why not just kill him?"

Mac shrugged. "There's nothing in the contract that says we can't. We're just to get the artifact from him."

Ezra leaned forward. "What kind of artifact are we talking about here?" He'd dealt with his share of artifacts over the years. Most of them were nasty pieces of work that were better off destroyed.

"A vampire artifact." Mac stared at the empty bottle like he was about to make it fly across the room for a refill.

Sly sighed and shook his head. "I don't like messing with vampires. You can't trust them."

"Sly, is it you can't trust them, or they see through you every time you've dealt with them?" Bloodclaw asked.

"It doesn't really matter." Mac interrupted before Sly had the opportunity to speak. "What matters is if we get this artifact, we can stop another coven from moving into Colorado."

"Right." Jefferson finished off his beer. "That I can get behind. This frontier used to be safe before the monsters started moving in after the war. If we can slow them down, I'm your guy."

"We're his guys." Bloodclaw patted Jefferson on the shoulder as if to remind him they were partners in every sense of the word.

Jefferson flashed Bloodclaw a smile. "We're your guys," he repeated.

Ezra had always liked the easy relationship the two had. Jefferson was a deadly monster hunter, and Bloodclaw was a powerful Sioux shaman. He wasn't sure where they'd met, but he'd known them for about ten years. They were always together, and dead monsters tended to show up wherever they went. They might appear to be hard, dangerous men, but around those who knew them, they were completely devoted to each other. Ezra was always too focused on his magic to worry about romantic relationships, but if he ever stumbled across one, he hoped it was as honest and happy as what the two men had.

"Okay. So, when does this go down?" Ezra liked knowing exactly when and where he needed to be.

"Tomorrow night." Mac reached for the empty beer bottles on the table.

"Cutting it a bit close, aren't you?" Sly frowned and finished off his beer.

"Yeah, I wish we had more time to plan." Mac snagged

Sly's bottle. "Unfortunately, my contact just found me last week, and it took me a couple of days to track you guys down, contact you, and give you time to get here."

"You're lucky we were in Colorado Springs after killing a wererat who was trying to take over a whorehouse there." Bloodclaw cleaned his fingernails with Jefferson's distinctive chipped bowie knife. Jefferson always claimed the big chip along the back side was from when it got stuck on the rib of a zombie buffalo. Bloodclaw never disputed the tale. He was always subtly borrowing Jefferson's things in a casual way that reflected the depth of their relationship.

"No luck involved. You should remember I don't believe in luck." Mac lined the empty bottles up on the table. "I checked to see who was within reach and selected you accordingly. We've got to get into place tomorrow. We don't have a lot of time. From my information, the vampire will be traveling by coach from Lamar."

"Why don't we hit him during the day?" Ezra figured Mac was about to begin using the beer bottles to explain the layout of the vampire's caravan. He hated the idea of attacking a vampire at night. "He's a vampire. That would be safer."

Mac shook his head. "Can't do it. It might be safer for us, but not for the artifact. That's the big reason he's not traveling in a light-proof coach by day. The artifact is so sensitive to light that it has to be kept underground during the day. If we try to move it in the daylight, it explodes. So, we track him by night, get the artifact, and get it to safety before the sun comes up."

Ezra shook his head. "This doesn't make sense. What artifact are we after, and if it's a vampire artifact, why are we protecting it?" He didn't like the idea of not knowing what they were actually doing. He spent most of his time wandering from place to place dealing with the creatures that could devastate the human population if they were left to their own devices. Every so often someone contacted him to do a special job. But those jobs normally involved taking out covens of vampires, or packs of werewolves when towns felt threatened by creatures massively more powerful than humans. Most of the time he worked solo. The rare occasions he'd worked with others, things ended badly for at least one member of the crew. If he had to pick one member of this crew to lose, it was Sly.

"I wasn't told," Mac picked up one of the bottles. "But the money's good enough, I'm not asking any questions."

"No," Sly snapped. "This sounds like we're working for vampires, I don't like that. We're supposed to kill vampires, not work for them."

"That's what we've all done for years," Mac said. "The man I talked to wasn't a vampire, but there was something mysterious about him."

"And you didn't scan him?" Ezra tapped the table. "That's not like you, Mac."

Mac shook his head. "No, I scanned him. He was shielded from any psychic or magical reading. He was a blank slate."

"Nobody's a blank slate." Bloodclaw handed Jefferson's knife back to him.

"That's why I knew he was shielded," Mac said.

"To be shielded against you, he's very powerful." Jefferson sheathed his knife. "If he's that strong, why isn't he going after this artifact on his own?"

"Maybe you can ask him after we get the artifact," Mac said.

Ezra wanted to back out of the deal. He didn't like the idea of working for a powerful person that was bold enough to want a piece of vampire history. Those things were always dark and covered in blood. Maybe he could work something out to balance things, to stop the bad guys from winning.

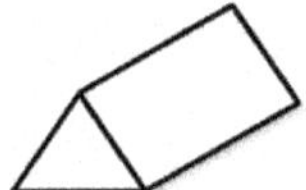

The saloon was out of rooms, so Ezra had to ride several blocks to find a place. It wasn't the best place in the world, but he was happy to find a spot that got a roof over his head. The door creaked slightly as he opened it. If that was the only problem with noise he was going to have that evening, he was good with that.

As he closed the door, something moved in the shadows. With practiced ease, Ezra had his six-shooters in his hands, each pistol glowed as he pumped magical energy into them, ready to blow whatever it was to smithereens.

"Whoa there, Ezra." Sly struck a match and lit the oil lamp

beside the bed. "No need for the weaponry there."

"Why not?" Ezra let the spells around his pistols fade but made a slow cautious show of putting them back into his holsters.

"We're on the same team." Sly settled back on the threadbare chair he'd been sitting in when Ezra walked in. "Working together and all that."

Ezra frowned. "I'll give you that we're on the same team, but I don't like working with you." He walked over to the bed and sat. It creaked and smelled musty. Not the worst bed he'd ever slept in, but not the best by a long shot.

"Ezra, we used to be friends." Sly gave him a look that on anyone else's face would have been one of innocence, but on Sly, it made Ezra wonder what his angle was.

"That was years ago." Ezra unbuckled his gun belt and started to hang it over the bedpost. That would put it a little farther out of reach than Ezra liked with Sly around. Instead, he laid it on the bed, with the handles facing him. "You betrayed my trust and I don't like putting myself at risk like that again."

Sly shook his head. "We all need to let the past go and focus on the future. This vampire isn't going to be easy to deal with. You know that, don't you?"

Ezra snorted and pulled off his boots. He wiggled his toes, happy to be out of the confining leather. "It's a vampire. Vampires are never easy."

"Right, but I get the feeling there's something Mac isn't

telling us."

"We all keep our secrets; that's how we work." Determined not to let Sly think he could make him uneasy, Ezra lay back on the bed, his back against the scratched and stained headboard. He also didn't want to let Sly know he'd known Mac wasn't being completely honest with them back at the saloon.

Sly stood and paced at the foot of the bed. "I've been reading the cards every night since I got Mac's summons. There're secrets inside of secrets with this one. There's also someone actively working on blocking me from seeing what's coming."

It was all Ezra could do to keep from laughing in Sly's face. "Sly, you're a charlatan at best, and a downright fraud at worst. I'm not sure why Mac recruited you for this job, but he did, and I have to work with you. I'd much rather not have to tie you up and leave you in this room, which, how did you find me anyway? I didn't even know where I was going when I left the saloon."

Sly stopped pacing and glared. "I'm not as much a charlatan as you think." He spun on his heels and headed for the door. "When this job goes to hell, just remember I tried to warn you." He yanked the door open and stormed out.

Ezra let out a long, relaxing sigh. The room felt a lot nicer with Sly gone. Just his involvement was enough to make Ezra want to pack up and leave, but Mac had pulled his fat out of the fire a couple of times, and the first time, Ezra had given him a favor for it. Mac had never cashed in that favor, and Ezra was worried if he didn't help out, Mac would call it due, and he'd have to do the job, whether he liked it or not.

Dust from the trail mingled with the steam from Mac's wagon and Ezra's storse. Ezra wished there had been some rain to settle the dust, but the blue sky hadn't produced rain for months, if the locals were to be believed. Not that Ezra had any reason to doubt it. The landscape looked ready to blow away in one huge dust storm.

He rode on the far side of the wagon from Sly. Ezra felt more comfortable keeping the extra distance between them, even though he knew there was little chance of Sly trying anything until after their job was done. That was Sly's pattern. Do a job, then do his best to make sure things turned out better for him than everyone else.

They were making good time, not even slowed down by Sly's horse. He was the only one who actually rode one. He had less magic and was also less prone to run into things like werewolves and zombies, that tended to scare livestock.

"We should make it by dark," Mac called down from the front seat of his wagon. Bloodclaw was next to him with Jefferson in the back seat, near the smokestack belching steam. The wagon itself was a major marvel, bright and shiny with lots of intricate details cast into the metal body. In many ways, it was like a gypsy wagon, without the horses. One time, many years earlier, Ezra had tried to study all the figures and symbols there and failed miserably. When he'd asked about them, Mac had simply explained he'd worked with the engineer who built it and had a lot of magic woven into it, along with the latest in steam-powered gadgetry. It had lots of lights, umbrellas, a portable campfire, several adjustable steel defensive shields, a Gatling gun and a flame thrower. If he wasn't taken by surprise, Mac could hold off a horde of zombies or small pack of werewolves all by himself.

"I think so," Bloodclaw replied. "The signs are favorable. I don't foresee any problems."

"Fortune telling is supposed to be my forte," Sly complained.

"Then you should've said something before I did," Bloodclaw said.

"Mac, you need to talk to your tinker friends and see if they can invent a self-driving storse," Ezra said, wishing he could simply point his metal steed in the direction he wanted to go, cross his arms, and go to sleep, content in the knowledge his horse would wake him if there was a problem, but then a storse had no way of detecting danger. Ezra always figured he could find a way to modify a ward spell to act as an early warning system.

Mac laughed. "Don't I wish. Of course, if they could do that, most of us traveling wizard sorts would be on the road all the time, traveling through the night, in every blizzard and sandstorm."

"Don't make us sound like the post office," Jefferson said with a yawn. "Besides, most of us are on the move all the time anyway. I don't remember the last time Bloodclaw and I had more than a couple of nights in the same saloon, or even the same campsite. Sometimes I think we're destined to become the walking dead just from pure exhaustion."

"We deliver people their safety, not the mail," Mac said then chuckled. "Although, I'm sure the pony express would love a self-guiding storse, or something similar."

Bloodclaw nodded. "My people might actually embrace that technology. So far, the Sioux have resisted your white steam. Unlike some of our eastern tribes." There was a note of disdain in the big Indian's voice. A night several years earlier, Ezra had managed to sit and talk to him around a campfire. He and many of the others from the western tribes didn't approve of how wholeheartedly most of the eastern tribes had embraced the white man and their technology. Even being partnered with Jefferson didn't change Bloodclaw's opinion of the people moving west and bringing disease and monsters with them. He was a shaman and able to hold his own against the invasion when it personally impacted him, but he and all of the other shamans couldn't keep their tribes completely safe and it was a prickly subject with a man who won nearly every battle he fought, but knew he was losing the bigger war.

"Next time I talk with my engineer, I'll get his mind working on the project," Mac said. "If he knew the Sioux nation might be customers, he might find a way to make it happen. Most engineers can use the extra cash."

"You whites are always looking for a way to make a profit." Bloodclaw crossed his arms and frowned.

"Sure thing," Mac replied. "Gotta keep us going."

As they rode along the dusty trail toward La Junta, they dropped into the conversation they often had when more than a couple of them were together, the reasons whites relied more on steam than magic to live their lives while the Indians were determined to live their lives the way they had for thousands of years. Ezra didn't add much to the conversation, mostly keeping his well-known opinions to himself. He agreed with Bloodclaw on a lot of things and unlike Mac and Sly, understood that native magic was better than Anglo spells in The West. He'd seen people pull off some pretty spectacular things east of the Mississippi, but that area had been tamed more than The West had, and he doubted The West would ever be brought to heel the way The East had been. If he had his way, he'd never cross the great river again, but he didn't always get his way. The universe was good at throwing him curve balls, so he never made promises he wasn't sure he'd keep. He kept ending up doing things like dealing with vampires, and that was always a good way to find himself unable to keep promises.

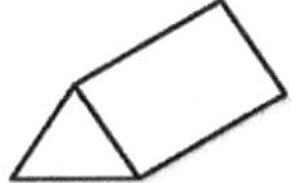

Ezra followed as Mac turned off the road and headed out across the prairie. He didn't see any signs of human habitation, but since they were after vampires, there didn't need to be any human habitation around. There could be a canyon with a series of caves, or maybe the vampire they were after had just gone to ground for the day.

"Over there." Mac pointed to a wagon parked near a clump of junipers. He stopped his wagon behind a boulder and out of sight of the vampire's transport.

"What's the plan?" Sly asked as he tied his horse to a brass ring on Mac's wagon.

Mac glanced at the sun in the western sky. "We've got about an hour. Let's make sure their wagon isn't going to leave here."

Ezra got off his storse, then took a moment to get his supplies out of the locked boxes designed to look like saddle bags on its flanks. He had a decent supply of iron wood bullets, specially designed to be fired at vampires. They were just as effective as a stake through the heart, but even with his magical gun, he had to make sure to hit the monster's heart. If he missed the heart, he'd just piss it off. That was the drawback of shooting at the things, but it was better to shoot one several times from a safe distance, than to grapple with it up close and personal. He slipped on a bandolier with more bullets as well as vials of holy water, garlic oil, and a concoction he was dying to try out, bottled sunlight. He and another mage had been working on it for a while and hadn't had a good excuse to use it. Sure, he'd run into vampires since the last version was perfected, but they hadn't been doing anything wrong at the time and he'd let them go. Theoretically, it would also work on zombies, but most necromancers tended to avoid the uncivilized west. They appeared to be a stuck-up bunch. He slipped a couple of wooden knives into the pouch on his gun belt, just in case something got past all of his defenses, and he had to go hand-to-hand.

"You about done over there?" Mac asked. "We're burning daylight." He was also more battle-ready than he had been during the ride out from Pueblo. He had a bandolier similar to Ezra's, along with a sleek sword sheathed at his waist.

"Sure." Ezra walked over to where the others were standing, looking toward the wagon by the juniper. "Mac, you still haven't said what the plan is after we disable their transportation."

"We're going to back off a bit and pick them off as they come out of the ground." Mac led the way across the prairie to the wagon. "If we're lucky, they'll be disoriented and easy targets."

Sly huffed. "Not that I mind easy money, but if this job is going to be as simple as you make it sound, why did you need all of us along with you?"

Mac huffed. "You've said it yourself, there's something about these vamps that makes it hard to read what they're about to do. I want as many people at my back as possible. Too many things can go wrong. With the vampires' speed, I need folks who can help balance things out."

"So we're cannon fodder," Sly mumbled.

"You might be cannon fodder, but we're not," Jefferson said. "We're backing Mac up and doing what we can to make sure everyone comes home alive."

Ezra took a couple of steps away from the group to avoid a large clump of yucca plants. The place was so prickly and pokey that if fighting got overly physical, the vampires wouldn't be the only things hurting them. He'd do his best to make sure it didn't come to that.

When they reached the wagon, it was much more impressive than it looked when they spotted it. The big metal box was nearly three times the size of Mac's wagon. It was easily big enough for a dozen people to ride inside while the driver sat in the seat up top. The carvings were elaborate, and at first just looked decorative until Ezra studied the hunting scenes and spotted arcane symbols mingled in. If he hadn't known what to look for, he'd have missed it completely.

"Careful, there's more than a little bit of magic in this baby." He cautiously touched one of the less dangerous symbols and traced it with his finger. A sharp shock rewarded him for his efforts.

"We'll let you set off all the traps," Sly said from a few feet back.

Mac tried the door on the side of the wagon closest to Ezra. It didn't open. "Looks like they've locked it. Let's get to work breaking their magics. Sly, while we're working on the more delicate job, see if you can get the wheels off this beast. Even if we can't get into the engine, if you get those off, it won't go anywhere."

Sly frowned and put his hands on his hips. "Do I look like a blacksmith?"

Jefferson clapped him on the back. "No, and neither do I, but since I don't have magic like the other guys, I'll lend you a hand. I'm used to being the muscle in the family." He smiled at Bloodclaw and then went off and started pulling limbs off the juniper bush, bending them over his knee, and throwing the ones that broke aside.

Ezra studied the symbols, trying to figure out how to bypass the many magical traps he spotted in the wagon's decorations. If he was right about what most of it meant, there were some pretty nasty spells guarding the wagon.

"This might not be easy to disarm." Ezra stepped away from the wagon and frowned. "Got any extra salt in your wagon? I didn't bring any."

Mac nodded. "What are you thinking?"

"If we can't disarm this thing in the time we've got, maybe we can imprison it in a circle." Ezra started walking around the wagon, not happy with the uneven, rough land it was parked on. It would make creating a strong, stable circle difficult at best.

"It's a good idea," Bloodclaw agreed.

"I'll go get the salt, you two work on this." Mac turned and hurried back the way they'd come.

"Nasty blood magic went into this." Bloodclaw pulled out his wand. Ezra had seen it a few times before. It was a large piece, particularly to be carrying around while he and Jefferson were on the trail most of the time. He didn't even know if the two of them had a permanent home, although he figured Bloodclaw had a place in one of the Sioux clans. The wand was topped by a huge quartz crystal held in an eagle's talon. As much as he wanted to, Ezra hadn't spent much time studying the thing. It was rude to pry too deeply into another magic user's spells and tools, unless they offered, or if they were a teacher. Bloodclaw wasn't his teacher and had never offered to let Ezra study his stuff, so Ezra kept his hands and eyes to himself.

"I agree, and I'm not good at breaking blood magic." Ezra caressed the pearl handle of his six shooter. He liked his magic more direct and less invasive than blood magic tended to be. He also didn't like having to rely on sources of power outside himself. With blood magic, too much could go south.

Bloodclaw shook his head. "Me either. Foul, rancid stuff."

Muttering something in Sioux or some other native language Ezra didn't understand but vaguely recognized, Bloodclaw shook his wand at the wagon. He made a complete pass around it as Jefferson and Sly came over carrying a couple of large limbs. Without stopping his shaking and chanting, he gestured at Jefferson, who put a hand up for Sly to stop. When Bloodclaw got back to Ezra, he shouted something and pointed the wand. A blast of magic blazed out of the huge crystal and hit the side of the wagon. The wagon rocked violently, but when it stopped, appeared undamaged.

"Yeah, this is some really strong, nasty work." Bloodclaw tucked his wand back in his belt.

"Is it safe for us to try to pull the wheels off?" Jefferson asked.

"Yes." Bloodclaw responded. "Wait. Let me check for spells on the wheels."

"I'll take the back." Ezra headed for the rear of the wagon. He couldn't imagine anyone putting booby traps on wheels, but he'd never encountered anything with this level of blood magic on it before.

As he knelt beside the right wheel, something exploded from the front of the wagon. Ezra straightened and ran for the front. Bloodclaw sat on the ground ten feet from the wagon. His rawhide leather jacket smoked from several places and both Bloodclaw and Jefferson were patting out the flames on Bloodclaw's left sleeve.

"You okay?" Jefferson asked as they got the flames out and Ezra reached them.

"Going to need a new jacket when we get back to town," Bloodclaw grumbled. "But otherwise I think I'm intact. Ezra, be careful checking the other wheels. There could be similar explosives there, or I may have set some kind of auto defense spell off with my more direct assault earlier."

"Yeah, that was smart," Sly mumbled. "Not sure we should even try to get the wheels off this thing if they're going to explode each time."

"The one I disarmed shouldn't be a problem again." Bloodclaw shot his singed sleeve a hard look and headed toward the other front wheel. "If we're lucky it was the only one that will do that."

Ezra wasn't so sure he wanted to mess with the rear wheels, after what the front one did to Bloodclaw, but it would've been worse if it had hit either Jefferson or Sly. They didn't have the same level of magical protections he and Bloodclaw had. He was part of a team. He had to do his part. He went back to the wheel he'd been about to check.

Standing several feet behind the wagon, Ezra sent out a feeler of magic. The overall magic of the wagon made it hard to tell if there was anything specific around the wheel. He opened his mind to the magic around the wagon. It made the wagon glow red in his vision. The illumination around the wheel was softer than the rest of the wagon. Ezra pushed against the magic and the glow faded even more.

Another explosion rocked the wagon and the whole thing tilted.

Ezra ran to the front of the wagon.

Bloodclaw was sitting fifteen feet from the wagon, pulling

cactus quills out of his hands. The wheel on the right side was gone. "I don't think it's going anywhere."

Jefferson had thrown down his branch and was reaching for Bloodclaw to pull him up.

"Guess we don't need to take off the other wheels," Sly said, leaning on the branch he'd found.

"This wagon ain't going nowhere," Jefferson said.

"Don't need this now," Mac held up a bag which Ezra assumed was the salt he'd gone looking for.

Ezra shook his head. "No, let's use it to set up our defenses. We weren't expecting the wagon to have these types of protections. It's possible we might be dealing with a vampire mage."

Sly frowned. "I didn't sign up for anything like that."

"I think if we're dealing with a vampire mage, we need to take them down even more." Mac handed the salt to Ezra. "We don't want a vampire mage here in The West. The regular ones cause enough problems."

"That might explain this artifact you told us about." Ezra opened the bag of salt and scanned around the area, trying to find a decent spot to set up a defensive circle. Then another idea hit him. "Bloodclaw, what do you say about setting up two circles for us to stand in? If we position ourselves correctly, we might be able to trap the vampires between us."

Bloodclaw glanced toward the horizon where the sun was beginning to set. "It's a good idea, but we'd better move fast."

He came over and took off his hat to let Ezra pour salt into it. "I'll go over behind the wagon. I can't exactly tell where they're going to come up from."

"Let me help," Sly held out his hat too. "I guess you want one right here? For three people, so fifteen feet across?"

Ezra paused before doling out salt to Sly. He didn't like the idea of him helping but had to admit it would speed things up. With the shadows lengthening, they didn't have much time. "Start over there." He pointed to a spot about fifteen feet from where he stood. "Go clockwise and end up where I'm standing here. Join the two lines seamlessly, or we're going to be in big trouble."

Sly huffed. "I do know how to do a secure circle."

"This is vampires we're dealing with," Mac reminded them before Ezra could say anything. "The circles can't be too secure."

That was Ezra's concern too. He didn't want anything to go wrong. The longer they were on the job, the more he realized they didn't know enough about what they were facing. The wagon screamed blood mage. They had no idea exactly how many vampires they were dealing with, or what the artifact they were supposed to retrieve did. He walked the circle, carefully making sure he dumped enough salt on the ground to have a completely tight circle. Any spot where the line went over a barrel cactus or other obstacle, he made sure to dump extra salt there, making the line heavier, but obscuring any imperfection the plant or rock might cause. He hated having to use salt on the ground, it always left a dead spot that might take years to come back.

When he reached the start of Sly's part of the circle, he glanced over as Sly finished up his section. "Need any more salt to flesh it out?" Ezra had enough salt remaining in the bag to fill a few holes.

"Nah." Sly shook his head. "I'm good over here."

"Ezra, get this thing up." Mac carefully entered the circle. "We've got visitors."

Even as his words faded, the first hands reached up through the soil near the wagon.

Across the way from them, Bloodclaw shouted something and magic danced across Ezra's senses. It was raw, without most of the subtlety Bloodclaw's spells normally held, but he didn't have time for subtlety, and neither did Ezra.

With a glance at the growing twilight, Ezra called on the strongest source of power he could tap into, the universe itself. They had no way of knowing if the vampire mage had done anything to contaminate the energy of the earth they'd slept in. The only way he could sense a pollution of it would be to tap into it, and he didn't want to, so he reached out to the stars that were growing in brightness. The power burned into him. Ezra turned his thoughts to the salt circle he, Mac, and Sly stood in. He forced that cosmic strength into the tiny crystals around him. To his mage sight, they sparkled like tiny stars themselves, then coalesced into a dome of power. It took a little extra effort to make sure their spells and bullets would pass through the barrier without bringing it down. In the end, Ezra created the magical equivalent of a fort that would be nearly impossible for the vampires to breach.

"Wow." Mac walked over and put out a tentative hand to the shield. "That's impressive. I'd say you've been working on that for a while."

Ezra took a deep centering breath, leveling out the power racing through him. "A bit. It's all about tapping into the right power source."

"I didn't know you had that much in you," Sly's tone was uneasy for the first time and it sounded like he was up to something.

"Here they come!" Jefferson shouted from the circle on the other side of the wagon.

Mac made a fast series of sweeping gestures that ended up in a point. A bolt of magical power blazed out of his hand and struck the first vampire rising from the dry earth. The monster screamed and went up in a plume of fire, like it had been hit by sunlight.

As if in response to their comrade's death, the earth between the two circles exploded as the rest of the vampires left their earthy beds at once.

A dozen angry vampires stood glaring at them.

"Okay, I wasn't expecting this," Mac muttered and began

casting another spell.

"Twelve of them, five of us." Ezra whipped his six shooters free of their holsters. "Could be worse." He fired, taking down two quickly with clean shots through the hearts, even with the dust still settling from their arrival.

Then the wagon door opened.

A bolt of magic slammed into Ezra's shield. It hit hard enough to stagger him. He turned his attention from the vampires who'd just risen, to the one jumping out of the wagon with another dozen flowing out after him.

The vampire looked like a dapper Southern gentleman with a dark evening coat, matching slacks and shiny boots. His short blond hair was perfectly groomed, as was the rest of him.

"You broke my wagon." The vampire flung a bolt of power at Bloodclaw. When it struck, Bloodclaw's shield lit up like a bonfire, then faded again.

"We don't want you in The West!" Mac shouted as his next volley of magic flew toward the vampire mage, the one obviously in charge of the other vampires.

If there was a more powerful vampire with them, Ezra didn't want to find out. He fired at the mage, hoping either his bullets or Mac's magic would get through.

With a wave of his hand, the vampire blocked Mac's spell. Ezra's bullets ricocheted off, catching one of the other vampires in the shoulder and sending him to the ground with a scream. Even if it wasn't a heart strike, his ironwood bullets would still cause it pain.

"If this one is the leader, take out the other ones," Mac suggested softly as Sly fired his own gun. "It will weaken its power."

If nothing else, Mac was good at coming up with spur-of-the-moment plans. Ezra nodded. "Sounds good." He changed his target from the one who appeared to be in charge and started picking off the less powerful ones. His gun glowed bright as he forced magic through it to improve his aim, hitting many of the vampires banging against his shield like crazed zombies. The leader stood off to the side and kept hurling bolts of magic, alternating his attacks on Ezra and Bloodclaw. As they took out the lesser vampires, the blows from the mage grew weaker.

"Running out of bullets here," Sly said.

Ezra pulled off his bandolier with one hand and tossed it to Sly. "Here. If you were a better shot, you'd still have plenty."

"Yeah, whatever." Sly slipped the weapon's belt over his head.

Turning his attention back to the vampires, Ezra caught the moment when Bloodclaw's shield fell, leaving him and Jefferson defenseless. With a roar that would do an enraged grizzly proud, Jefferson charged the vampires rushing toward him. He had his huge scimitar out and swinging. The blade glowed with its own power. The vampires slowed and spread out to encircle him.

Although they still had a few bodies throw themselves against Ezra's weakening shield, Ezra knew they had to help

Jefferson. He took out one of the vampires with an almost impossible shot between two vampires pounding on his shield.

"Damn, that was a good shot," Sly said. "I bet this holy water of yours will make these fools back off." He pulled a couple of the vials off the bandolier and lobbed them at the vampires."

Ezra reacted too late. "Not the holy water, you fool."

The vials hit their intended targets, but the water splashed back against Ezra's shield. It sizzled as it hit. If the shield hadn't been weakened, the effect wouldn't have been so dramatic. Ezra would've been able to patch it as the blessed liquid did its job, but the vampire mage had already done too much damage to it. While Ezra had been busy shooting his followers, he'd weakened their protections to the point the splash of enchanted fluid ate away at the shield.

"Fools." The vampire mage sneered. "Humans are useless, except to be consumed." He cast another bolt of power and took a step forward as if to steady himself.

Reflexively, Ezra blocked the spell that would've hit Sly. Since he'd been using his pistol instead of his magic, he was still strong enough to block the attack, although it hit hard enough to put him on his knees.

Turning his pistols on the new target. Ezra fired, hoping he had enough ammo, so he wasn't going to need to reload from his gun belt before he finished off the vampire. The vampire blocked his attack with magic, then stepped forward.

"The yellow vials!" Ezra shouted at Sly. "Throw the yellow vials." They hadn't had time to test the bottled sunshine, but if they worked as well as predicted, they should make a major impact on the vampire.

Sly yanked one of the yellow vials from the bandolier and hurled it at the vampire. In the ever-darkening sky, the vial glowed yellow as it tumbled end over end toward its target. The dapper vampire moved as if to get out of the way, but the vial caught its coat tail. The impact was enough to shatter the vial and send the yellow goo inside flying out everywhere.

The vampire yowled like a cat and started shaking its hand. Where the goo hit, yellow smoke rose up, and within seconds, rays of yellow were blasting through its skin.

"Time to die!" Jefferson shouted as he cut off the vampire's escape. He swung his curved sword in a huge arch and lobbed the vampire's head off.

Several of the other remaining vampires turned and ran off as little more than blurs in the night.

Ezra fired two shots that blazed through the night and took out two more vampires before they were out of range.

"Remind me not to piss you off," Sly said, sliding his pistols into his holsters.

"Too late." Ezra put one pistol away but kept out the other one. It didn't feel right, almost like the fight had been too easy. He huffed. As badly as he wanted to curl up and sleep for a while, it hadn't been that easy of a fight. The last time anything had broken his magical shield it had been a giant along the Platte river up near the Continental Divide. He'd been in a major fight then, and it didn't feel any different, except the ground was dry and not snow-covered.

"Hey, you could've warned me about the holy water," Sly objected.

"Yes, I could have, if I'd known that's what you were going for. The rest of us were shooting. Okay, Mac was slinging spells. What made you think lobbing vials was going to be a good idea?" Ezra walked among the downed vampires that hadn't disintegrated when they died. It all depended on how old a vampire was as to what it did when it died its final death. Young would often have to be reburied. There were only four bodies, and Jefferson was busy cutting off heads to make sure nothing would come back to bite them in the asses.

With nothing left for him to do, he joined Mac at the open door of the wagon.

"Think we should try to go in?" Mac was studying the door frame closely.

"You didn't find the artifact in the dust pile that had been the mage, did you?" Ezra squatted down to check the threshold for anything out of sorts. There were a series of arcane symbols there, like other places on the wagon, but the piece of wood there wasn't as ornately carved as the rest of the wagon, it was just a simple piece of oak with symbols shallowly engraved and then painted to blend in. Most people wouldn't have noticed them.

"The only things he left behind were his fancy clothes and a bit of jewelry." Mac tried to push his hand through the door, but it resisted him. He didn't yelp or holler in pain, but his frown deepened. "We can go through it all later. Might be something there for an added bonus to the job."

"So we get to keep the loot?" Sly asked from a short distance away. "You didn't say anything about that earlier."

"Our contract is just for the artifact." Mac moved a couple of steps away from the wagon. "Ezra, give me a little room, I want to try something."

Ezra wasn't about to stand around while Mac did anything that might cause the wagon to explode or rebound magic at them. He hurried over to where Bloodclaw and Jefferson were standing and watched what they were doing at the wagon.

"He's going to get us all blown up, isn't he?" Jefferson asked.

"I hope not," Ezra pulled off his hat and wiped his brow with a handkerchief. "I don't know about you two, but I think I've got a lot more living to do."

"With you there," Bloodclaw said. "We might want to get shields ready, just in case."

"I love the vote of confidence, guys," Mac grumbled, and his hands glowed as he started working a spell.

Ezra called the energy to erect a shield at a moment's notice. Most simple, non-dangerous spells didn't cause hands to glow as they were cast. Mac was doing something major. It made sense. They were dealing with blood magic, and major firepower was needed. Having seen what the wagon could do to protect its wheels, and after glimpsing the protective symbols on the doorway, Ezra wasn't going to take any chances.

Mac's spell hit the wagon. It wasn't a simple hit and dissipate spell, the magic hit and poured out of Mac into the doorway. The wagon resisted. The shield flared nearly sun bright. It thrummed with so much power, the ground under Ezra's feet vibrated. Then Mac's spell went through. It cracked the shield and went all the way through the wagon, punching a hole in the far side.

As he dropped the power to the spell, Mac stumbled and fell to his knees next to the wagon. "That was one powerful shield."

Bloodclaw rushed over and knelt at his side. "No, my friend, that was one really strong spell you just cast."

"I call it an extended battering ram," Mac said softly, then sat in the dust. "I think I'm going to sit here for a couple of minutes while you guys go check the wagon out."

"Any idea what this artifact looks like?" Ezra dropped the magic he'd been holding for the shield and walked over to the wagon.

Mac shook his head. "I didn't get a description. He just said to look for the strongest magic in the area."

Sly frowned as he jumped up into the wagon's open door. "That could've been the wagon, or the vampire mage himself."

"No." Mac took a deep breath. "I was assured it was

something we'd be able to carry back."

Bloodclaw handed him a water skin. "Here, drink this. It'll help revive you."

Calling up a bit of mage light, Ezra followed Sly into the wagon. The inside was as opulent as the exterior. Instead of intricate carvings intertwined with arcane symbols, it was decorated with lavish silks. The furniture was elegant with embroidered silky cushions. There weren't any lights in the place, and the mage light muted the colors to the point Ezra was sure the place would be absolutely breathtaking in full sunlight, although it probably never actually saw that kind of exposure.

"Powerful magic," Sly muttered as he went over to a small desk. "If I was a bunch of vampires traveling cross country, where would I hide powerful magic?"

"In an unlikely place," Ezra said moving past Sly and deeper into the wagon. "Although with the wagon's defenses I doubt they were worried about being robbed."

"We are uniquely qualified for that, aren't we?" Sly gave up on the desk and started tossing pillows off the nearby couch.

"Yes, we are." Ezra opened himself to the feeling of magic and did his best to ignore the amount of dark power rolling around the wagon. He didn't want to spend all night acting like a common bandit by destroying more than he had to.

Two beacons of light glittered in his magical sight. They were close to each other, but vastly different. One dark and dangerous, the other was light and welcoming. Without a word to Sly, Ezra opened a door in the wagon's entry room. A spring on the door swung it closed with a soft click. Ezra tested it to make sure it hadn't locked him in. The knob still turned easily. The back room wasn't as lush, although it was easily twice as large as the first room, and Ezra figured the steam engines that powered the wagon were most likely located behind the door across from him. He paused and looked at what he was about to walk across. Cushions lay scattered around the room. They looked more like small, overstuffed mattresses. He'd never seen a vampire's den look like this, but then he'd never heard of vampires sleeping the day in a wagon. They always went to ground unless they were in their coven house, and then they still slept in the basement, safely away from the sun.

The cushions radiated magic, but it was fading, obviously something the vampire mage had created and when he died, his magical creations did too. That realization gave Ezra a shiver. The defenses on the wagon hadn't diminished with the vampire's death. That meant someone else had crafted them. He wasn't sure he ever wanted to meet anyone that strong in blood magic. Wanting to get the artifact and leave, Ezra looked toward the corner his sight told him the magic came from. Two wardrobes stood in the far corner. The dark one on the right and the light one on the left.

"Okay, that's an odd arrangement," Ezra mumbled to himself as he waded across the cushions, hoping the vampires hadn't left any kind of physical traps he might stumble across.

He was reaching for the dark cabinet when Sly opened the door. "Nothing in the main room. I had to get Mac to make more mage light after you left with yours. You find anything in here?"

"I'll tell you in a couple of seconds." Ezra touched the wardrobe. The blood magic there was thick, like sticking his hand into warm molasses. It pulled at him and sought to crawl up his arm.

Ezra stepped back and tried to shield himself before he touched the piece of furniture again. On the second try, the magic tried to take him again. It was alive in its death aura. The feeling of it on him made him want to take a long bath in a cold mountain stream where the running water could dilute it and wash it away. He stepped back again. "There's something here. Have Bloodclaw come see what he thinks, unless Mac is up to it. It's powerful, and dangerous."

"Okay." Sly turned and rushed out of the wagon.

With his departure, Ezra turned to the light cabinet. It didn't attack him when he touched it. Its power was strong and gentle. There was no indication that it was going to try and swallow him whole. Not letting down his guard, Ezra opened the wardrobe and stared in.

A young man cowered in the cabinet's corner. He was naked and shaking.

"Who are you?" Ezra asked. There was no way he was a vampire. The undead didn't give off light magic the way this young man did. He seemed to have a natural magic about him.

The young man looked over his shoulder cautiously. The movement brought him deeper into Ezra's mage light, revealing the scars on his neck, shoulders, and back from bite marks. Some of the ones on his back looked like they might be lashes from a whip or riding crop.

"You're not a vampire." It was a statement, not a question.

Ezra shook his head and held out a hand to the young man. "No. I'm a man. A spellslinger."

The young man looked confused. "Spellslinger?"

"Yes." Ezra kept his hand out to the young man. "A mage who uses magic to hunt monsters."

"Did you kill them all?" The young man shifted and moved toward Ezra. "The vampires, are they all dead? Even Wayne?"

Ezra frowned. What kind of name was Wayne for a vampire? "If he was the mage, then yes, even Wayne. A couple of them escaped, but we got most of them."

The young man eased forward and took Ezra's hand. From as slight as he looked in the wardrobe, the size of his hand surprised Ezra. It was larger than his own, and he wasn't a small man. Ezra pulled the young man from the wardrobe and when he was standing outside it, he was slightly taller than Ezra, though not as tall as Jefferson. He was willowy and delicate. There was something about him that said he was more than human. He had nearly no body hair, like an Indian, but was pale like a white man. Then he moved his head and his long, unkept hair moved to reveal his ears.

"You're an elf." Ezra said a bit louder than he'd meant to.

"An elf?" Sly came back in. "Who's an elf?"

A scared look appeared on the elf's face. Ezra patted his hand. "It's okay. He's a friend. He's one of the ones who helped defeat the vampires."

The elf relaxed but continued to keep hold of Ezra.

'Whoa, is the elf the artifact?" Sly came closer with Bloodclaw, Jefferson, and Mac in tow.

"An elf," Mac stepped around Sly. He still looked a bit wobbly, but his eyes were clearer than they had been outside the wagon. "I've heard about them, but never actually seen one before."

"Let alone a naked one," Jefferson added with a note of appreciation in his voice.

For some reason, that tone irritated Ezra.

"Looks like the vampires have been feeding on him," Mac said. "That's not good. I don't know if elves can become vampires, but with the amount of light magic he's putting out, I think I know where that vampire mage was getting some of his power."

"Wayne," Ezra corrected.

Mac's face wrinkled in confusion. "Who's Wayne?"

"Wayne is… the vampire mage, or at least that's what the elf says." Ezra turned so he was standing in front of the elf. "You haven't told me what your name is. I'm Ezra."

The elf smiled and made Ezra's heart pound furiously.

"Tholomasie."

"Tholomasie?" It was an odd sounding name, but Ezra figured if he was an elf, that might explain it.

"Most humans, and vampires just call me Tom."

"Tom's a lot easier to say." Ezra turned to the guys. "Alright everyone, this is Tom, the elf. Tom, this is Sly, Mac, Bloodclaw, and Jefferson." He pointed to each man as he named them.

The men made appropriate greetings, then Mac walked over to the wardrobe extruding dark magic. "Yeah, this is a nasty piece of work too. These vampires just keep getting darker and darker."

"What do you want with the idol of life?" Tom asked.

Mac turned to him. "Idol of Life? Is that what this thing is? We were hired to acquire it."

"Wait a minute," Bloodclaw put his hand on Mac's shoulder. "I've heard of the Idol of Life. There are supposedly several of these things spread out across the world. They become the center of the vampire community wherever they go. They are part of the original curse of the vampires."

Mac's eyes grew wide as a knot formed in Ezra's stomach. "Original curse?" Ezra asked. "As in when the seven original vampires formed an eternal pact to one day rule the world? That original curse?"

Tom nodded. "Yes, that original curse. The thing that created the blood feeders that are the bane of your world and mine."

Mac turned from the wardrobe. "So, that's true too. Elves aren't from this world."

"We live in a parallel dimension from this one. Vampires are one of the few creatures from this world that can easily traverse the boundaries between the worlds." Tom sighed and leaned against Ezra. "Unfortunately, they have a taste for our blood. The vampire mages especially enjoy it. Our light nourishes their darkness."

Tom's weight against Ezra was almost nothing and Ezra found himself wanting to protect Tom. Without thinking about it, he put his arm around Tom's waist, drawing him closer. Tom didn't object.

"Mac, I don't like that you haven't come clean about who we're working for here," Ezra said, an unbidden growl entered his voice. He didn't want to hand over a vampire idol to vampires.

"We have a chance to rid our world of some of the darkness," Bloodclaw said. "We should destroy this thing. Now. If we let it out of our hands, who knows what problems we'll be creating?"

"I'm with Bloodclaw on this," Jefferson said, taking off his big top hat and running his hand through his brown hair. "We can't just let this thing continue to do its magic."

"Who cares if the vampires keep this thing, or someone else gets their hands on it," Sly countered. "We were hired to deliver it to someone, and we need to honor that contract. Right, Mac?"

Mac stood there with a puzzled look on his face. He rubbed his cheeks and then walked outside without a word.

"He is your leader?" Tom asked, turning slightly, but not moving out of Ezra's hold.

Ezra nodded. "He is, or at least he's the one who called us all together for this."

Bloodclaw pulled a tomahawk from his belt. "I don't care what Mac wants at this point. He's not been totally open with us on this. I've sworn an oath that means more than white man's money." He stepped up to the wardrobe. "I must do what I can to keep The People safe, and this idol is a danger to us all."

As he swung the tomahawk at the cabinet, the weapon glowed with bright yellow light. For a moment, it was like the light that had come from the other wardrobe, where Tom had been. The tomahawk nearly hit the wardrobe. Darkness flared in the wagon. Bloodclaw flew across the room and hit the far wall hard enough to shatter the thin paneling there before sliding down to the floor.

"Bloodclaw!" Jefferson rushed across the room and threw himself on the floor next to him. "Bloodclaw, are you okay?"

Bloodclaw moaned something.

"Well that wasn't the smartest thing in the world to do," Sly said as he touched the wardrobe doors. "This thing obviously knows how to protect itself from brute force attacks."

"Then we need to find another way to get it opened." Mac

walked back into the room. "As much as I don't like the idea of tarnishing my reputation as someone who can get things done, I think you three are right. We don't need to let this thing back out into the world." He walked over to the wardrobe and bent down to look at it. "I don't see any markings on it for protections." He glanced over his shoulder at Tom. "Do you know any way into this? You've been here for a while."

Tom pursed his delicate lips, then pointed at Sly. "He can open the doors."

Ezra and Mac stared from Sly to Tom and back again.

"Sly? Sly can open the door?" Ezra was fairly sure he couldn't have understood Tom right. Sly didn't have enough magic to be able to open the door. There was no way.

Tom nodded as he stepped out of Ezra's arm and up to the wardrobe. He reached out to touch it but failed to get even as close as Bloodclaw's tomahawk had. The cabinet pulsed darkly where Tom's hand was but didn't flash with the intensity it had with the shaman's attack on it.

"The idol repels light." Tom stepped away from the wardrobe. "I think that's why they kept me so close to it. To torment me when they weren't feeding on me." He returned to Ezra's side, and without thinking about it, Ezra put his arm back around the elf's bare waist. It felt right to try to protect him.

Ezra chuckled. "So, you're saying Sly doesn't have as much light in him as the rest of us do?" It was nice hearing someone else confirm what he'd suspected for years."

"I just understand when things don't have to always be for the greater good." Sly mumbled and reached for the small brass ring that served as the handle on the door. He pulled the door open.

Darkness rolled out of the cabinet. Ezra drew power and forced it into a shield. Tom blazed with his own light. For several moments, the elf's light and the idol's darkness fought silently for control of the wagon, then the darkness retreated to the idol and Tom's intensity died back.

The idol sat on a stone pedestal in the middle of the wardrobe. It didn't look like much. More of a phallic symbol than what Ezra would've expected a vessel of darkness that helped create vampires should've been. It also looked to be made out of wood. Ezra wondered if there was more to it than that. He'd never heard of wood, not even ironwood, holding the amount of power the idol had.

"Death to death," Mac mumbled.

Sly reached into the cabinet and touched the idol before lifting it from the pedestal. The way he moved it easily, it must not have weighed a lot. "It doesn't look like much."

"Many powerful things, don't look like much." Bloodclaw hobbled closer, leaning heavily on Jefferson. "Now that it's free of the wardrobe, take it outside so we can destroy it."

"Good idea," Mac said. "Maybe if we all hit it at once, we can break the magic and blow it up like a keg of TNT."

Ezra wasn't real sure he wanted to be around if it went up

like a keg of explosives, but after pulling down one of the silk curtains to use as a robe, he led Tom out of the wagon and onto the moonlit prairie.

Tom stopped and took a deep breath as they cleared the wagon. He closed his eyes and smiled. "It's been so long."

"So long since what?" Ezra was afraid he already knew the answer but wanted to hear it from the elf. His need to kill vampires grew.

"Since I've been out of that wagon. They let me out of the ward…my cell, every night, so they could feed from me." Tom took another deep breath and seemed to get lighter than he had been moments before. "But they kept me shrouded in their blood magic. It's been years since I saw the night sky. I can't wait to see the sun."

"Hey guys, this thing's smoking." Sly held the idol out, glancing about as if trying to figure out where he could put it.

Mac pointed to a rock near where Ezra had created his circle of protection. "Over there. I was told it was sensitive to any level of sunlight. I guess moonlight qualifies."

"So we could just wait and let the sun destroy it," Jefferson said as he helped Bloodclaw sit on a nearby boulder.

Bloodclaw shook his head. "No. We destroy it now. Any vampire within hundreds of miles will feel its power being extinguished. It will send a message to them. They will leave."

Jefferson patted his shoulder. "Do you have the power? You look pretty wasted."

"We can handle it," Mac said. He still looked grim. "Ezra, if you and Tom can lend me a hand."

"Tom?" Ezra looked over at the elf at his side.

"Of course." Light blazed again from Tom. Being out of the wagon, it was brighter, almost a miniature sun. The idol smoked more, as if the smoke would protect it from the light hitting it.

Ezra used a light spell of his own. He didn't think it was sun-bright, but it added to the idol's torment. As he thought about what the vampires had done to Tom, keeping him captive, feeding from him, not letting him out of their hellish wagon, his light grew stronger.

Mac's bolt of magic hit the idol. A long crack appeared in its side. Ezra reached up for the stars as he'd done when he was casting his circle. As smoke poured out of the widening gap, Ezra shoved more light into the crack. The dark smoke pushed against the light, but the damage grew wider.

With a flick of his hand, Mac hurled another magical bolt. It struck the idol and it flew off the rock, as it traveled through the air, the dark smoke grew dense enough to block the wagon from view. The idol hit the ground and darkness exploded out of it.

Ezra tried to shield from the darkness, but it was too much. It hit him hard and threw him against the side of the wagon. Something else thudded next to him. His head spun. He fought to push back at the darkness, but it overcame him.

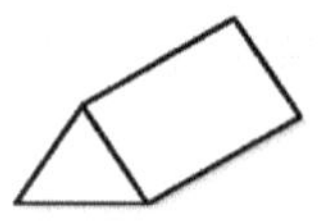

The sun coming over the horizon was so bright, Ezra blinked against it. His head pounded and he wasn't sure if it was from the magic, or the sunlight.

"Ezra." Tom sat on the ground next to him. He wasn't naked anymore, although the clothes he wore hung awkwardly from his narrow frame. "You're back with us."

"Wow." Ezra eased into a sitting position. "That was some punch. Did we break it?"

Tom smiled. It was nearly as bright as the rising sun. "Yes, we broke it. The Idol of Life is no more."

"I think if we find another of those things, we need to be a little more careful," Jefferson said from nearby. Bloodclaw was sitting on a boulder like nothing had happened, but if the sun was coming up, they'd all had enough time to recover from the magical assault.

Ezra glanced around. Mac was a few feet away, leaning against the wagon wall that he'd apparently been slammed against along with Ezra. He looked okay as he sat there drinking from Bloodclaw's canteen.

The only one who wasn't in sight was Sly.

"Where's Sly?" Ezra took a water skin Tom offered him.

"No clue," Jefferson replied. "Obnoxious bastard took off before any of us woke up. It's almost like that blast of darkness didn't affect him."

"There's enough darkness in him, it might not have," Tom said.

"Last time I hire his ass to do anything," Mac grumbled. "I'm betting he was lying about something blocking his visions of how the job was going to go."

Ezra shook his head. "I've always doubted if he even has magic." He handed the water skin back to Tom. When they got back to his storse, he'd break out trail rations, unless Mac had thought to bring enough for everyone in his wagon.

"He's got magic," Mac said getting to his feet. "It's just not as active as the rest of ours. Most seers are more passive. I wouldn't have hired him for the job if he couldn't have added something to the team." He dusted himself off. "I just didn't expect him to run out on us like this."

"Not the first time, probably won't be the last." Ezra accepted Tom's hand to help him to his feet. The world moved slightly as his head spun and he leaned a little more against Tom than he expected.

"Probably right there," Mac grumbled. "Let's get back to town. We won't get paid for this one, but I'll spot you guys for a bath and a night in Pueblo."

After they decided to destroy the idol, Ezra wasn't expecting to get paid. He hoped they got into town in time to find Tom some clothes that actually fit. They were also going to need to talk and figure out what they were going to do with the elf, but that could wait until they were all cleaned up and had a good meal in their bellies. He wasn't sure how much scrubbing it was going to take to get the Idol of Life darkness off him, but at least they were all in one piece. He was always happy when he went up against vampires and got out of it without losing anything.

S. R. Battle

S. R. Battle has been a member of Colorado Springs Fiction Writers Group for 21 years. She's almost a Colorado native, having lived in the area since she was about two years old. As a kid, she used to have competitions with her older brother to see who could write the weirdest, grossest, funniest story or poem. She's a published poet and writes abstract poetry because that's how her brain works. Her true love is the thrill of good story telling. There've been several freelance editing adventures in the past. This is her first anthology.

Robert Brownson

Originally from Traverse City, Michigan, Robert Brownson has had a life-long loving involvement with literature. After majoring in English at the University of Michigan, he went on to receive a Masters in English at the University of Colorado and then a Ph.D. in Comparative Literature. After twenty years of teaching English, Latin, French, and computer programming, he joined MCI in 1994 and stayed with the company for twenty years until he retired from Verizon in 2019. He is now writing some science fiction and making whatever contributions he can as an editor.